"What a voice."   —AMY TAN

"Offers a funny yet heartfelt answer to the question 'What happened to the one that got away?' "   —LIBRARY JOURNAL

"Wry, brutally honest . . . liberating laugh-out-loud passages. There are also moments of heartbreak and kindness . . . which are all the more potent for their understatement."   —PUBLISHERS WEEKLY

"[A] hilariously brash protagonist . . . This impossible-to-put-down novel is a gripping, emotional roller coaster much like the highs and lows of pregnancy itself."   —THE SEATTLE POST-INTELLIGENCER

"Mary Guterson is witty, wily, and wonderful." —KAREN JOY FOWLER, author of THE JANE AUSTEN BOOK CLUB

"A simply wonderful, hilarious, heartbreaking book. Guterson had me from the first page and there was no putting it down."
                            —MARK SALZMAN, author of LYING AWAKE

"A gracefully imagined and bluntly expressed novel, a rare combination. It speaks directly to the heart about the heart, also rare and very welcome."   —KAYE GIBBONS, author of DIVINING WOMEN

"Wryly witty . . . darkly comic . . . [a] quirky, irreverent debut."
                                                              —BOOKPAGE

"A brisk and irreverent romp through the panic fields of contemporary marriage. Mary Guterson is wickedly, bruisingly funny. Her characters may be uncertain about, well, almost everything, but there's nothing they're afraid to tell us."   —ROBERT COHEN, author of INSPIRED SLEEP

"We Are All Fine Here is never judgmental, always irreverent, a sardonic, gimlet-eyed look at life at its messiest, the way most of us live it whether we mean to or not."   —FORT WORTH STAR-TELEGRAM

We are
all fine here

Mary Guterson

BERKLEY BOOKS, NEW YORK

THE BERKLEY PUBLISHING GROUP
Published by the Penguin Group
Penguin Group (USA) Inc.
375 Hudson Street, New York, New York 10014, USA
Penguin Group (Canada), 90 Eglinton Avenue East, Suite 700, Toronto, Ontario M4P 2Y3, Canada
(a division of Pearson Penguin Canada Inc.)
Penguin Books Ltd., 80 Strand, London WC2R 0RL, England
Penguin Group Ireland, 25 St. Stephen's Green, Dublin 2, Ireland (a division of Penguin Books Ltd.)
Penguin Group (Australia), 250 Camberwell Road, Camberwell, Victoria 3124, Australia
(a division of Pearson Australia Group Pty. Ltd.)
Penguin Books India Pvt. Ltd., 11 Community Centre, Panchsheel Park, New Delhi—110 017, India
Penguin Group (NZ), Cnr. Airborne and Rosedale Roads, Albany, Auckland 1310, New Zealand
(a division of Pearson New Zealand Ltd.)
Penguin Books (South Africa) (Pty.) Ltd., 24 Sturdee Avenue, Rosebank, Johannesburg 2196,
South Africa

Penguin Books Ltd., Registered Offices: 80 Strand, London WC2R 0RL, England

This is a work of fiction. Names, characters, places, and incidents either are the product of the author's imagination or are used fictitiously, and any resemblance to actual persons, living or dead, business establishments, events, or locales is entirely coincidental. The publisher does not have any control over and does not assume any responsibility for author or third-party websites or their content.

PRINTING HISTORY
G. P. Putnam's Sons hardcover edition / January 2005
Berkley trade paperback edition / February 2006

Berkley trade paperback ISBN: 0-425-20767-6

The Library of Congress has registered the G. P. Putnam's Sons hardcover edition as follows:

Guterson, Mary.
    We are all fine here / Mary Guterson.
        p.   cm.
    ISBN 0-399-15230-X
  1. Pregnant women—Fiction.   2. Married women—Fiction.
  3. First loves—Fiction.   I. Title.
  PS3607.U79W4   2005   2004044352

PRINTED IN THE UNITED STATES OF AMERICA

10   9   8   7   6   5   4   3   2   1

For Rob

No one is better at rewriting history than my mother. My mother takes all the stories she wants to forget and simply disowns them, shrugs them off, acts as if they belonged to someone else. For instance, she now claims to have never raised her voice with my father in all of their married life (I was there; I heard her), to have never spent a summer wearing that ridiculous wig to hide a bad perm (we have pictures), to have never lost me in the shoe department at Marshalls when I was six (major trauma of my childhood). In my mother's revamped universe, none of it happened.

If only I'd inherited my mother's gift of revision.

How nice to be able to pretty up the shabbier details of my life, to dispense with the more embarrassing fuck-ups. How refreshing to continuously begin with a clean slate. But I can't do it. Even if I'd been born with the knack, my mistakes won't disappear so easily.

Case in point: I'm pregnant. Which wouldn't be such a fuck-up, I suppose, if only I were younger, happily married, in better shape, didn't have to work, weren't worried about the teenage son I already have, and had some kind of inkling as to whether the father is Ray or Jim. But as it stands, I'm a bit of a mess.

Relationship Test #1:

A couple lived together on an island off the coast of Maine without electricity, telephones, or running water. They had no children, no newspapers, no car accidents, no Seventh-Day Adventists leaving religious literature on their doorstep, no neighbors who turned out to be child molesters. In fact, they had no neighbors at all. They had only each other. They built their house by hand. They grew their own vegetables, heated their place with wood. For supplies, eventually one or the other would row to the mainland and stock up. They lived this way for years and years, until the husband died of pneumonia. Without phone lines, the elderly wife had to wheelbarrow her sickly husband to the beach and flag down a passing ship.

Pick one:

A. This is a love story.

B. This is a horror story.

I blame all of it on Ray. If only he'd had the common sense and the good grace to stay away and leave me alone. I'd been doing all right. I'd grown accustomed to my Rayless life. It helped that he'd moved to another state. It helped that I never saw him anymore. It helped that the reality of his existence had shrunk over the years to the sporadic phone call, a distant voice looping through the old, overplayed sound track of our old, played-out love life. That and the few thousand daydreams I'd created where the two of us, miraculously, got together again.

And then, last September, he called because after all the years of living together Melissa and Greg had finally decided to get married and he wanted me to come with him to the wedding. Everyone would be there, he told me. All the people I used to know.

Come on, he said.

Why did I take him up on it? Why didn't I see how stupid it was of me to think we could actually be a couple of mature adults—older, wiser, slightly cynical former lovers laughing lightly at former jokes, separately sighing with relief that we'd broken things off in the nick of time? I guess I've always been a bit of an idiot when it comes to Ray.

Even though my period is at least two weeks late, and maybe even three (why, oh, why can't I be one of those women who keep track of such things?), and even though I've already peed over a pregnancy stick not once, but twice, and both times elicited the same little blue bar that means one thing and one thing only, that thing being that nothing will ever be the same as it was prior to the appearance of that defiant little blue bar, and even though I'm already feeling somewhat queasy at the smell of garbage and I gag every time I brush my teeth and have suddenly lost the ability to eat most anything but frozen macaroni-and-cheese dinners with tater tots on the side, I can't stop myself from purchasing one more little urine stick, just to be absolutely and positively certain that I really and truly am with child. Because mistakes do happen. I remember when my sister, Stacy, thought that she was pregnant (tested pregnant, in fact, by her very own doctor's test in her very own doctor's office) and then, two weeks later— poof!—it was gone. Disappeared. Dissolved back into her body, into her bloodstream. The old embryonic disappearing act. That could happen to me, right?

So I buy another urine stick from the Rite Aid across town where no one knows me, and I stop at a McDonald's across the street and head for the women's rest room, where I pee over the stick, hovering above the disgusting McDonald's toilet seat, holding my breath the whole time to keep from gagging on the stench of the McDonald's women's rest room, and then I wait the full minute I'm supposed to wait, standing alone in the loneliest stall in the universe only to find out that, as I had suspected, I'm not alone after all. Someone else is with me, floating in amniotic fluid. There are two of us in the stall in the McDonald's women's rest room, but only one of us, as far as I know, feels an urgent need to throw up.

For the first time in as long as I can remember, my therapist does not shrug. On the contrary. His eyes grow wide; his eyebrows rise. His head moves a shade forward toward me. I believe he may actually be showing emotion, although of what type I can't be certain. Then he shrugs.

Yeah, I say. Pretty hard to believe, huh?

[Shrug]

I mean, how dumb of me, right?

[Shrug]

My therapist's office smells as if he used the room during off-hours for planting medicinal herbs—all peat moss and fresh dirt and something slightly alcohol-tinged, like cough syrup. It's a smell I've grown accustomed to, a smell that brings me comfort. Which is a good thing, considering the fact that my therapist is not at all what you'd call comforting. He says next to nothing, week after week. Just sends vague, incomprehensible messages through the various degrees of height he manages to reach in the raising of his shoulders in his continual shrugs. Over the years I've devised methods to squeeze a drop more of a reaction out of him. Talking about my sex life usually wakes him up. Talking about my mother or other tiresome topics sets him to making obvious glances at the clock on the wall behind me. Crying gets him to lean forward and hand me a tissue.

I start to cry. He hands me a tissue.

I can't believe this, I say. I mean, I do believe it, but I just can't believe it.

He shrugs and purses his lips. Because he has a bushy mustache, this lip pursing makes his bottom lip disappear beneath a fringe of grayish hairs. He looks grandfatherly. He looks too old to be hearing my sordid tales. I worry about him. He leans forward to hand me another tissue. He glances at the clock behind my head.

I'm so stupid, I say.

He says nothing.

Later, at home, I pour the last of my precious Klonopins out onto the kitchen table and try to see if there is a message in the design they create. Klonopin tea leaves. There seems to be no pressing message other than "Wipe the table better next time." I scoop the Klonopins into a pile and attempt to draw some wisdom out of the tiny mountain they become. I ask the mountain: How many of you would it take before I lost consciousness forever? Are there enough of you to do me in? Or would I end up in a vegetative state, drooling uncontrollably, the hairs on my chin left to propagate like fields of poppies until even my neighbor Gwen won't come to visit me anymore? How shallow is it to not kill yourself because you're afraid of what you'll look like in near-death?

I brush the pile of Klonopins into my palm and march them to the toilet. They settle innocently on the bottom of the bowl. When I flush them down, it's not without a rain of regret washing over me, leaving me soaked to the gills.

There's nothing lower than sleeping with a man who is not your husband. I know this. I know I haven't got any good excuses for my behavior. I can't even use the lousy-husband defense, because in truth, my husband isn't all that lousy. He's fine. Just fine. Totally fine. A completely and utterly fine husband. Mr. Husband.

As my mother, the revisionist, used to write me at summer camp: We are all fine and hope to hear the same from you.

I will attempt an explanation.

You know how sometimes you hear about people taking an innocent-enough stroll down the sidewalk? Maybe they needed a moment of fresh air, or perhaps they just that second ran out of cigarettes, or maybe they remembered in the middle of a meeting that it's their wedding anniversary and they'd better go purchase some flowers or jewelry quick before landing in the doghouse for the fifth year in a row, or whatever. There they are, walking down the street, taking in the air and the sounds and the smells, and letting their mind wander a bit and maybe even saying to themselves in that exact moment how happy they are to be alive, maybe even thanking the good Lord above for giving them this one moment of pure happiness, maybe in that same moment telling themselves that this is what life is really all about, these singular moments when one feels totally at peace, so much so that they feel like thanking the Lord, but thanking him silently inside their own head, because it's really not a part of their makeup to be shouting thanks to the Lord on a city street, or even mumbling it lightly, they're not crazy or anything. And just as they are set to move on from that thought and come back to reality and remember their anniversary or the meeting they are missing or the fact that smoking really and truly does do a major number on their lungs and they promise promise promise that after buying this last pack of cigarettes they really and truly will finally do something about their goddamn smoking habit—right then and there, in that moment before their thoughts can even begin to make the inevitable switch from thanking the Lord to recalling all of the mundane, depressing details that daily haunt them and make their lives small and difficult, it suddenly happens: An air conditioner decides to decamp from its precarious perch on the ledge of a fifth-floor windowsill to fall fall fall fall down down down down, landing smack-dab on their head, smashing it in, forever and ever releasing them from any further mundane thoughts and instead taking them to that place of profound whatever-it-is that we all will someday be more than familiar with. You've read about this type of thing happening, right? Because if you *have* read such a thing, and if you then stopped for a moment and thought about how the future is filled with shit that we won't know about until we get there, and if you also felt a sudden panic over the thought that anything can happen, at any time, and if in that moment you also felt a rush of something indescribable in your gut, a rush of recognition of your own future out there waiting for you, whatever it is—if you have ever had any of these thoughts and feelings and rushes in your gut, then maybe you will know what it felt like the moment I first laid eyes upon Ray, deep into a game of Frisbee on the lawn in front of the Student Union Building. Shirtless.

* * *

Call me shallow. He looked good. He looked better than good. He looked beautiful. He looked like a gazelle, long and sleek, his hair tossed back from his forehead in the easy, careless way that all men with less hair wish for, his chest tan and hairless, his shoulders large and round, his pants hovering at his hips at that exact spot where belly ends and muscular groin begins. He might as well have been naked. He leapt between students eating their sandwiches, studying for tests in art history or logic or the culture of ancient Mesopotamia. He leapt and danced among them, his movements full of grace, his arms stretched out above him like a child reaching for candy, utterly free. His body spoke of air and space everlasting. He spun as if to show no ropes could tether him to earth. No rules applied. Nothing could bring him down. I should have seen it all then. Should have known that what he exuded spelled only ruin and heartache.

Look at that asshole, my girlfriend uttered, but it was too late. I've always been an idiot for a hairless chest.

I was eighteen years old. I'd slept with five boys in my life. Five slobbery, emotional boys with penises like slender sticks, and bodies like puppies, hearts pounding, soft tongues panting, breaths squealing in their small, momentary pleasures. They fell asleep like puppies, too. Deep, innocent, happy slumber, their bodies still twitching in remembrance.

But here was Ray, all grown up, his face faintly rutted with the creases that would eventually deepen over time, giving him an unwarranted air of wisdom. Here was Ray with his natural ease, his smooth stride, his strong, muscular arms, his perfect jaw. Here was Ray, the poster child for masculinity, prancing in front of me while I sucked down a Marlboro, hoping the fact that I'd just been hit by lightning at the sight of him wasn't completely obvious.

I spent the next couple of weeks eating lunch outside, furtively looking about for the Frisbee guy on the Student Union Building lawn. But he never reappeared. No matter. I had classes to attend, tests to take. I had a future awaiting me somewhere among the course listings of the university catalogue. Any day now, I'd find myself immersed in a major of passionate import. Any day now, I'd figure out what to do with my life. Who had time for a boyfriend?

Then some dork in my human sexuality course asked if I would mind returning a book he'd borrowed from a guy who lived in my dormitory—a request it didn't take a genius to see was only, in reality, a lame attempt at making conversation. The dork had been after me all quarter. But did he really think I'd go out with a guy who would try to make eye contact during discussions on masturbation statistics or the varying degrees of vaginal blood flow detected during experiments on visual stimuli? But because beneath my thorny exterior lurks a nice-enough gal, I told him, all right, I'd return the book, seeing as how I lived on the second floor of McCarty Hall, and the rightful owner of the well-worn copy of Carlos Castaneda's *A Separate Reality* lived on the fifth. I stuffed the book into my backpack and forgot all about it.

A couple of weeks later, in a startling fit of organization, I emptied the contents of my backpack onto the floor and came across the Castaneda. My initial response was to toss it into the trash. But then I reconsidered. Perhaps the owner felt some abnormal attachment to this particular book. Who was I to deprive him of its comfort?

I headed up to the fifth floor in a pair of ill-fitting shorts and an old, yellowing, hopelessly stretched-out polo shirt that had belonged to my father and that I had been sleeping in for the five years since he had died. Had I known I was about to face the love of my life I may well have reevaluated my wardrobe choice. Most of my hair had been in the same bun at the back of my head for more than a week, while chunks had come loose to fall in snake-like coils down my back. I looked terrible. I should have brushed my teeth, at least. But of course, I had no intentions of meeting anyone suitable, much less the man who would torture me for the next decade or two with passionate alcohol-infused declarations of love followed by total amnesia of same said declarations. No, I meant only to speedily pass off the book and hightail it back to my own dorm room, where a vast heap of wrinkled clothes covered the floor, awaiting their folded future. Then the door opened. There, to my simultaneous horror and delight, stood the Frisbee guy, fresh from the shower, his gleaming tanned body clad only in a skimpy white towel barely clinging to his perfect slim hips.

Yours? I said, holding the Castaneda into the space between us, a space I hoped was wide enough to dissipate the flow of breath emanating from my unwashed mouth.

Must be my roommate's, he said.

He looked me in the eye. Love at first sight: It happens.

Facts:

He was a geology major.

He was a skier.

He was a mountain climber.

For years after college, he lived alone in a mostly barren apartment. A bed on the floor, a few things tossed in the closet, a couple of cracked mugs in the cupboard. On one wall hung a map of the world with pins indicating the places he'd traveled. He'd been to places I'd never given a second thought to—Morocco for one, the Philippines for another. He'd been all through Europe and to India. He'd gone to South Africa with his father, and to Bermuda for a family vacation.

He'd made a small bundle selling marijuana to fraternities on campus.

He knew he had a nice chest.

He'd once slept with a married woman.

He was a surprisingly terrible kisser, but his slow, perceptive hands more than made up for it.

He enjoyed my tiny repertoire of topless dances.

He loved nothing more than a blow job in the afternoon.

He'd grown up in one of those quiet kinds of houses, a clean and empty place, with too much carpeting and too few pictures on the walls. His parents made me nervous. The first time I had dinner with his family, I kept waiting for the conversation to start, for someone to burp, or spill something, or tell about the funny thing that so-and-so had said that day at the office. But no one spoke a word. His sister never even looked up. You could hear the forks scraping against the plates. They asked one another to please pass the potatoes or the meat loaf, without a hint of irony.

Finally Ray said, Thanks, Mom, that was really good, and then he excused the two of us to go fuck in the basement bathroom while his mother did the dishes and his dad read the paper in the den.

* * *

It's amazing how far fucking can take you when you're barely twenty. It can seem like an entire relationship. We had a couple of good years together, fucking like crazy, followed by four really, really shitty years, followed by a decade and a half of regrettings, which pretty much takes us up to the present. What happened during those four shitty years was this: Ray kept meeting beautiful women. Beautiful outdoorsy women with long, straight hair and great collarbones and lean, wonderfully athletic legs who one by one opened those lean, wonderfully athletic legs to Ray. These women seemed to appear out of nowhere. Just when one had used up her allotted time another would show up, fresh and young and willing.

I made a few scenes. I fucked around myself, with a small slew of other guys. I cried myself to sleep a few million times. I hated his guts. I always came back. Always, always, always.

And then I got pregnant with Jim's baby and married him instead of Ray—a fact I've more or less never gotten over.

Not much of an explanation, I realize. I apologize.

If only I'd sent Melissa and Greg a hefty check through the mail instead of showing up for their ceremony. If only about a million things. Regret sucks.

2

It would be so much gentler on my psyche to blame my pregnancy on a drunken blur; a brief, instantly forgettable interlude; a moment so vague I may well have dreamt it. But I can do no such thing. I remember everything.

It's last October. Ray wasn't kidding. Everyone *is* at Melissa and Greg's wedding. My former life appears, like a mirage. Melissa wanders around in a slip, happily dazed. It's her wedding day and she's dopey and beautiful. The guests hover in small circles around the living room, catching up. The house is surrounded by trees and more trees, and in the distance even more trees. I try to not let the oppressive trees get to me. I try to ignore the fact that

I am standing a foot away from Ray. I try to act like a normal person.

I am carrying around a picture of my son as a conversation starter—proof that I've actually accomplished something in this life. What else do I have to offer for all the time gone by? My twelve years as a so-called paraeducator in the resource room at Thomas Alva Edison Intermediate School? I'm not even a teacher! I'm an underpaid babysitter of bratty suburban middle-school kids. And a lousy one at that.

Christy Williams traps me by the wine bar. I hardly recognize her. She's Melissa's maid of honor. She's put on a good thirty pounds since I last saw her. Her hair is cut in a tight wedge at the chin in a miscalculated attempt to create the illusion of more neck. She wears a peach-colored dress that does not flatter her curves in the slightest. Such is my peer group. We're all looking out of step these days.

Julia! she shouts at me.

I wave the picture of Chad in front of my face.

My son, I say.

Oh, he's darling! she cries.

Thanks.

He looks exactly like you!

This is not true. Chad looks nothing like me. He is the spitting image of his father, though of course no one at the wedding knows that. No one here has ever met Jim. No one here can imagine me with anyone other than Ray.

Soon I have a little group gathered around, everyone looking at the picture of Chad. Ray stands to my right, smiling as if he were the proud uncle. I slap him across the chest with the back of my hand.

Should have been his, I hear myself say.

Everybody laughs, Ray included. We all laugh at my bit of hilarity, my poke at Ray's disastrous move in dumping me way back when, the big idiot, the stupid jerk, the dumbshit ex-boyfriend. Should have kept her when you had the chance! Should have had babies with her! Too late now! Ho, ho, ho!

He'd picked me up for this shindig. Pulled up in his truck in front of our designated meeting spot—the shopping mall parking lot midway between my home in suburbia and the wedding, at Melissa's parents' house, a good forty-five miles out of town—as though it were perfectly normal to be pulling up in his truck in a shopping mall parking lot in northern Seattle. As though we got together every day instead of never. I leave my car parked where it is and hop into Ray's truck, all at once sure that today of all days Jim will decide he needs to go shopping at the mall, where he will, naturally, find no other parking space but the one next to the car I am supposedly driving to some old friends' wedding.

I can't help staring at Ray at first. I have conjured up his face so many times over the years that it no longer makes sense to me the way other people's faces do. He has a nose, yes. And two eyes and a mouth and all the rest of the parts that make up what we think of when the word *face* pops up in our minds. But Ray's face doesn't register with me that way. Ray's face isn't even a thing. Ray's face is a verb, not a noun. Not to grind a concept into the ground, but Ray's face is more dream than reality. And seeing it now in the flesh throws me for a loop.

On the way to the wedding, he pulls a typical Ray: parks his truck on the side of the road, steps out, strips off his jacket and T-shirt, and changes into what passes for a dress shirt in Ray's world—a short-sleeved bowling shirt in a shade of tangerine that probably looks perfectly normal in southern California but that stands out in these parts like the solitary white guy in a gospel choir. Who isn't going to look at him? He takes his time fastening the buttons, the asshole, while I make a point of not watching. Ray never could pass up an opportunity to show me his chest.

We barely talk as we drive to the wedding. We listen to a country-western radio station and look out the window. Every once in a while, Ray looks at me and chuckles, as if each time he's surprised all over again to find me sitting there next to him.

So it's going all right with that guy, huh? he says to me.

Ray cannot bring himself to speak Jim's name. He calls my husband "that guy" or "your man" or, when he's feeling gregarious, "your old man." And he asks me if things are going all right, as though one day I might fess up to a disaster.

Yeah, I say. Things are fine.

Well, that's too bad, he says.

Ray likes to play this stupid game with me. The "When are you going to leave that guy?" game. It goes like this: Ray will call and ask me, "When are you going to leave that guy, anyway?" And I'll say, "I don't know." And then he'll sigh and tell me that letting me go was the biggest mistake he ever made in his life and that Jim is the luckiest guy in the world and that if things ever go sour between Jim and me, Ray will be right there, waiting for me. I used to not believe him. I used to think that the phone was going to ring and Ray would be on the other end, telling me that he had met the love of his life and was sorry to have bothered me all these years but was calling to say good-bye for good now, it was over, he was marrying someone else. But it's been years now, and he's still not married to anyone else, and he's still calling me when he thinks Jim's not around, and he's still asking me, "So when are you going to leave that guy?"

And every time he asks that question, I can't help asking myself the same thing.

* * *

I can't get over how different everyone looks. When did we all start to look so conservative? When did the change come—that moment when a great haircut goes from chic and hip to looking only like short hair on an old face?

You look great. That's what I tell myself. You look great. Still, it seems I must make a trip to the bathroom to check. I wander through Melissa's parents' house, searching for the bathroom. The hallway is covered with pictures: Melissa's smiling family, posing in front of mountains and monuments, on beaches and elephants and muscular horses, in kayaks with the wilderness as a backdrop. Everyone smiles from ear to ear, the girls with manes of wild blond hair tossed to the wind. Melissa's father could be a shorter, less rugged brother of Harrison Ford, clothed in khaki shorts and a hunting shirt in one picture, in a dashing black tux in another. Her mother is a natural beauty, posed on a big boulder, strong legs bent at her bony knees, long fingers swiping at an errant wisp of hair. They depress me, these smiling, good-looking folks. These people happy to be with one another.

I hide out in the bathroom for a while, trying unsuccessfully to get my hair to settle down. The bathroom smells bad, a mixture of somebody's nervous dump and a bottle of too-sweet perfume. After a few minutes, I can't smell it anymore. You can get used to just about anything in this life, I tell myself, sudden spouter of bathroom wisdoms. You can live through most anything as long as you have the right tranquilizers on hand. Too bad I am currently all out of Klonopins. I open the medicine cabinet and poke around. Nothing but old aspirin, ancient creams and lotions, a gummed-up razor. I check under the sink and find a sad-looking enema tube inside a beige plastic tub.

Too bad Chad isn't around to amuse me. My perfect son, Chad. Fifteen. Opens his window when he smokes a joint in his bedroom, thus sparing me the embarrassment of having to think of an appropriate response to his stoned-headedness. Very polite of him, if you ask me. Also, he flatly refuses to show the least bit of interest in sports, which drives his father totally crazy. Jim has only two topics on which he can converse, sports being one. (His lawn, believe it or not, is the other.)

But then I remember that Chad no longer finds it amusing to amuse me. He no longer finds his mother a suitable companion. He prefers to be anywhere that his parents are not, doing whatever it is that he is doing. That's more or less how our little family operates these days—each of us spinning out in a separate orbit, satellites at different altitudes. We were pretty close for a while there, Chad and me. We used to spend a lot of afternoons doing basically nothing together. Watching CNN and poking fun at the reporters. Making chocolate chip cookies and eating most of the dough. Playing Risk and getting a bit too serious about world domination. Except then he went and got hairy legs and started spending more and more time in his bedroom with the door shut, and before I knew it, our time together was kaput. I can't remember the last time he let me kiss him without pulling away as quickly as possible immediately after.

I give up on my hair. I put on more lipstick and smear it in with my fingertip. I'm dying for a cigarette, but no one smokes anymore, not even me. Since I can't smoke, I decide to drink instead.

The bartender asks me what I'd like. Way too difficult of a question. My mind goes blank. What do I drink? All the guests seem to be holding a glass of the same red-tinged concoction.

I'll have whatever they're having, I tell him.

I am a highly suggestible person. I once worked in a gift shop with a woman named Claire, and this Claire showed up one day wearing a low-cut V-neck top, and right there, dead center on her chest, were two black hairs, just sitting there for everybody to see. Two big, black hairs. It was weird. Why would Claire wear something that revealed her two secret black hairs? And this Claire was a nice dresser, mind you. Classy dresser, all trousers-and-matching-blazers-and-shoes sort of thing. Anyway, the next morning—and I kid you not, it was the very next morning—I had sprouted two of my own. Really. In the exact same spot. Mine were wispier than Claire's, but you couldn't deny the fact of their existence. I plucked them right out, but can you see how suggestible I am?

And one night, a guy on television was talking about how his heels all of a sudden went numb on him, and despite the fact that I leapt out of the closet where I was searching for something to wear, and slammed off the television set, I'll be damned if I didn't wake up the next day with two frozen heels.

And then there was the time my husband suggested we get married.

To my great relief, the wedding ceremony isn't outdoors. Melissa and Greg are the outdoorsy types, always setting off on some horrifying journey involving bikes or backpacks or climbing ropes. In my former Ray-life, I tried to be outdoorsy, too. But I never really cared for any of it. Some people would rather look at mountains than climb them. Some people don't even mind if the mountain they are looking at is only a picture of a mountain. Those would be my kind of people.

Melissa is still in her slip, which turns out to be her dress. Silly me. Her shoulders are tiny and pink. Bits of blond hair fall out of her bun and curl around her face. She is a vision of innocence and light. Greg, who has been asking her to marry him for about ten years now, waits for her at the front as the guests gather in a sort of semicircle in the living room. I'm desperate for a chair but there aren't any. We are standing guests, some of us standing in the hallway. My feet ache from the cramped pair of heels I somehow persuaded myself to wear. Melissa, meanwhile, is barefoot.

Ray stands next to Greg, looking for all the world like a sun-drenched god in his tangerine shirt and khakis and leather sandals. He even has a tan, which no one else at the wedding has, since the rest of us still live in this rain-soaked corner of the universe. Tan Ray. His teeth are bone china. The hairs on his arms are bleached white against his skin.

Melissa and Greg begin to recite the vows they have written themselves. Fortunately, I am standing too far back to hear them. Their words of professed devotion float off into the atmosphere like the feathery seeds of dying dandelions. They stand facing each other, clutching hands. A string of white flowers streams down Melissa's back. She is radiant with love, with light, with promises.

My own wedding was nothing like this. My own wedding took place at a judge's house, with an old episode of *Star Trek* playing loudly on a television set in another room. The judge wore gray trousers and old brown slippers, scuffed at the toes. He had on a big sweater, the pockets stuffed with tissues. He had a bad cold.

All right, he said. You sign here.

I don't know what I was expecting. I suppose I thought you got at least a minute of something ceremonial in the package. Apparently not. Apparently what you get is a man blowing his nose loudly, and nearly—but not quite—drowning out the sounds of Captain Kirk asking for more engine power from Scotty, who in turn tells the Captain he doesn't think he can do it. And then the man who has just blown his nose points to the paper you are supposed to sign, which he then signs also, along with his grown son who has been called in from the television room to be a witness, and that's the whole thing. You are married.

This was followed up with a big party at my parents' house, which they insisted on giving. My mother called beforehand to ask if maybe I might wear something that would make my pregnancy less conspicuous, and I told her that might be a difficult trick, given that I was in my seventh month already.

I hope it's a girl, my mother said. I hope it's a girl who does to you the things you've done to me, and then you'll see what it's like.

* * *

I went to the doctor for the frozen heels. I asked the doctor, Is it a brain tumor? This was a new doctor, and I had made a pact with myself before going in that I would not cry in front of the new doctor, so I forced a little laugh when I said it, a laugh that ended up sounding as though I were choking on a chicken bone. I always cry at the doctor's office. I know I'm paying for it, but still, I feel so cared for. I'm aware of how pathetic that sounds. Pretend I didn't say it.

The doctor did not say that it was not a brain tumor. She said instead that it could be all sorts of things, but because she didn't specifically say that it wasn't a brain tumor, because she made a point of avoiding any reference to brain tumors and imminent death, I was convinced that was what it was. A big growing lump in my head.

The lab technician took blood from my arm, and I got all teary and told him that he was a prince among blood-takers, that I couldn't even feel the needle in my arm. He thanked me, but it was a hesitant thanks. The kind of thanks that means, "Please do not attempt to have a conversation with me." The kind of thanks that reminded me I was getting too old to say stupid things to cute male blood-takers. He slapped on a wad of cotton with a strip of medical tape and turned away.

A couple of weeks later my heels defrosted, and that was the end of it.

* * *

Ray nursed me through a few million illnesses. I've got to hand it to him: Barf never made him squeamish. Blood was just another liquid. A case of the runs was a funny, funny joke. When I had my wisdom teeth pulled, he took pictures of my swollen cheeks, which he still has somewhere, he says. Along with a few hundred pictures of me with no shirt on.

An hour into the reception, I am exhausted. They've all seen the picture of my son, and I've no choice but to tuck it back into my little black beaded evening bag—what was I thinking?—next to a pack of dental floss, a few crumpled tissues, and a tin of breath mints. It's an unusually warm afternoon for this time in fall. Pots of flowers loom everywhere, great bunches of color nodding in the indoor air, like crazy, half-drunk guests. All the people I used to know seem wholly content with the lives they've chosen. They stand around the living room, calmly conversing. No one appears desperate for something to say.

I spy around for Ray and locate him in the kitchen, chatting up some woman I've never seen before. The woman is laughing hard enough to give everyone within fifty yards a tour down her pink, waxy throat. Ray catches me glancing at him and does a quick double raise of his eyebrows, as though I should understand what that means. That was always the problem with our secret language. Neither one of us ever knew what the other was talking about.

A minute later, he finds me poking around the food table in the dining room.

Hey, he says.

I roll my eyes at him.

He laughs and steps close. He leans his face into mine and brushes his nose against my cheek. I stop breathing altogether. My existence shrinks, becomes only the feel of his skin on my face. How is it that he can still do this to me? He kisses me and I kiss him back. I know this kiss of his. I know this no-smell smell of his. Sweet and barely there. Instantly.

You're such an asshole, I tell him.

I admit to following Ray into the bathroom. I admit to standing behind him, my arms around his waist, my face pressed against his back, while he pees and then washes his hands (surprising me, I'll admit, with his newfound hygiene). I admit to the fact that in the old days, this was perfectly normal behavior: accompanying Ray to the bathroom, standing behind him with my arms around his waist while he pees. I admit to this behavior's being somewhat low under just about any circumstances, but in particular under the present ones. Sue me. I admit to all of it.

What I do not admit to is a total lack of hesitation when Ray turns around and kisses me again. I do hesitate. Okay, an extremely short hesitation perhaps, but nevertheless a high-speed trek through the possible consequences of continuing in the direction I seem to be headed. And during that short hesitation I admit to seeing only one roadblock, that roadblock being the fact that somewhere back in suburbia awaits my unsuspecting nuclear family—Chad and Jim. But I refuse to take their existence into consideration. That I also utterly fail to consider the penis–vagina–baby connection is beyond me. Hey, I never claimed to be a genius.

I would not like to be forced to count the number of times I've found myself uncomfortably fucking in somebody else's bathroom. What could be less appealing? There you are—feet hoisted skyward, cheeks perched on the hard, cold edge of someone else's sink just a yard or so from someone else's toilet, a mere spitting distance from someone else's damp hand towel, a few inches shy of the drawer that holds someone else's toothbrush and toothpaste and floss and gel and any number of other personal items, most of which are partially used and flaking or dried out or on their very last legs and ought to be disposed of, but which continue to fill the drawer despite the best of cleaning intentions—there you are, bouncing like a couple of Ecstasy-laden maniacs to the invisible beat of lust. A bathroom rave.

This time, I try not to think about anything. I try not to remember the sad-looking enema tube in the cabinet beneath me. I try not to think of the state of my frayed underwear, plainly visible on the bathroom floor. Instead, I tell myself to think about nothing, which, of course, never works. Nothing always turns into something, in this case the something being the stark reality of Ray's hurried breath against my forehead. When it's over, Ray smiles at me as though we have just successfully pulled off the biggest heist in the history of bank robbery. Goddamn, I love his smile. I smile, too, in truth a bit horrified but mostly only amazed at my sudden and complete lack of moral backbone.

That should have been it. Nice wedding, nice reception, nice afternoon together reliving old times, one semi-discreet bathroom fling for auld lang syne, good-bye forever, see you never, go away and leave me alone, bring on the credits, the outtakes, the best boy, the gaffer, the closing ballad, the filmed on location, the no-animals-injured-in-the-making-of-this-story disclaimer, the end of the whole damn thing.

Instead, it's going on Christmas and I'm sick as a dog, munching on saltines, contemplating the universe on the one hand and the many various types of suicide on the other, while all along the cells inside me multiply madly.

3

For a week now—ever since I found out for sure that I'm pregnant—I've been unable to concentrate at work. Stupid things happen. I drip coffee over my blouse. I can't find the keys to the resource room and have to ask the custodian to let me in. It takes a good five minutes of elaborate searching through my brain cells before I locate the password allowing entry into the school computer system. When I finally do boot up, the school calendar tells me I have just missed a required department meeting. Not that they'd actually fire me for such an infraction. Find someone else willing to work the resource room for the paltry salary they mete out to me month after month? I don't think so.

The thing is, I'm too freaked out to know what to do. Things would be weird enough without the biological mystery at hand. But the thought of having a baby hasn't occurred to me in years. I didn't even think I had the capacity for pregnancy anymore. I thought all my eggs had reached their expiration date. Jim and I go months at a time without bothering with birth control, unless you count abstinence, which, in truth, just about sums up our sex life.

Whenever I'm not crying or paralyzed with worry or practicing the various possible ways to let Jim in on the big, happy surprise, I mull over the options. For example, have a sweet brand-new baby—regardless of who the father is—and do a much better job with the parenting aspect this time. Watch that sweet little baby grow up to be a successful, happy, fulfilled adult who wants nothing more than to make sure that his/her mother spends her final days happily doing nothing, all the while surrounded by the nice material things she never had but always, on some shallow, conscious level, wished she did. Or have a sweet brand-new baby who turns out to have Down's syndrome, seeing as how I've reached the age where a Down's-syndrome baby is more than a possibility but practically a probability and with my luck a sure thing, and let that Down's-syndrome child follow me around for the next thirty years, give or take a decade, carrying my groceries and playing with the remote control and running into the street when cars are hurtling past in both directions until I lose my mind. Or have a baby with only one arm or one leg or half a brain or some terrible, horrifying early-childhood wasting disease and wonder what ever possessed me to bring such a helpless infant into the cruel, cruel world in the first place. Or abort.

So many options.

I give myself a short lecture. A Life Lecture. Buck up, I say. A lot of women your age would give their eyeteeth to be pregnant. You are blessed. You are fertile. You hold the secret to life in your very loins. So what if the paternity thing is a trifle ambiguous?

But I'm hardly listening. I didn't even remember to bring a pen to class.

Everywhere I turn now, there are screaming children. Everywhere I look, screaming children are plodding heavily in huge shoes, scraping hands along walls, making roaring-motor noises, picking their noses, dancing in place to personal sound tracks only they can hear. Everywhere I stand there happens to be a fresh-faced mother—looking way too young to be a mother—standing by my side, telling her small, chocolate-smeared child to hold her hand, stop touching that it can break, get over here right now, you're going to get a time-out when we get home, no you may not have a sucker, no means no, use your words, stop it now!

I don't know if I'm up to this.

I find myself sitting on the living room couch in the afternoons a lot, doing absolutely nothing. I have become very adept at this skill—nothingness. It's not all that hard. You simply stop moving. Sometimes, if I'm lucky, my acquired paralysis will lull me to sleep, thereby dropping the immobility bar even lower: a state of less than absolutely nothing.

The ironic upshot of my lack of movement is that, for the first time in as long as I can remember, my son notices me. A week or two into my couch-sitting/sleeping stint, he suddenly throws himself down in the chair across from me.

Ma, he says. Are you all right?

Fine, I say. Why?

Well, you've been sitting there spacing out for days now. It's kind of weird.

No, really, I say. I'm fine. Just tired, I guess.

I give what I intend to be a comforting smile, but which in reality looks more like a frown. I know this because it's exactly what my own mother does—frowns when she attempts to smile. Chad frowns back.

You sure you're okay? he asks.

I look at him for a moment, trying to come up with an adequate response. Is there a mother in the world who could do so? Since there seems to be no good answer to his perfectly good question, I fall back on what the experts do. I shrug.

I go to the library, seeking a place of quiet refuge from my living room couch.

Momentary truisms:

1. If you think the library might be a place of quiet refuge, think again.

2. If you happen to sneak a peek at the computer screen of the guy at the library who has asked you if you would mind keeping an eye on his things for a few minutes while he goes to do whatever it is he is going to go do, you will find the page filled with really bad, angst-filled poetry, making you unable to even glance in his direction when he returns from whatever angst-filled endeavor he has just returned from, and then you will feel guilty and also deeply depressed, knowing that everyone, everywhere, is filled with the same bad, angst-filled poetry that no one else wants to read.

* * *

For the millionth time, I consider quitting my job at Thomas Alva Edison Intermediate School. It's bad enough to have to witness the tortures of adolescence when you're not pregnant, but the constant up-close-and-personal reminders of what awaits me in the not-too-distant future if I am to bring this baby into the world are more than I can handle. Today smart-ass Jonathan excused himself to the bathroom only to come back an hour later with a safety pin stuck through his eyebrow. Who needs it? Still, no need to do anything rash. Rather than quit, I call in sick for a week and hang out with Gwen.

It's Gwen I decide to tell. She can bug the shit out of me, but most of the time I'm grateful for her friendship. Gwen and I can easily kill an entire afternoon waiting for something to happen outside our living room windows, knowing the chances of anything more interesting than watching our neighbor Eric uncomfortably toss a ball back and forth with his much younger, much cuter boyfriend in the middle of the street, hoping in vain thereby to fool his ancient mother, with whom he still lives, into thinking he's straight, are next to nil. And yet we wait. And while we wait, we tell each other things. Once, Gwen told me that she doesn't like to sleep with her husband, Bill, because he stinks. I loved her for telling me this sordid detail, even if it's exactly the kind of sordid detail you never want to know about another person.

When I spill the beans, I tell her only that I'm pregnant, and leave out the rest of it—the oh-by-the-way-don't-know-who-the-hell-the-father-is part. One piece at a time.

Well, Gwen, I say. Sit down.

What is it?

Let me ask you a question. What would be the absolute worst possible thing to happen to me right now, at this point, in this life that I'm leading?

Your mother's moving in with you?

Not that bad.

Your husband's having an affair?

Closer.

You have cancer?

Well, I do have a growth of sorts.

You have a tumor?

I'm pregnant.

Pregnant?

Pregnant.

Gwen's jaw drops. I watch as the blood flows upward from her neck, slowly covering her face like a mean case of hives.

No! she says.

Yes!

And then we both laugh so hard Gwen more or less pees her pants and has to run home across the street to change.

4

I take entire responsibility for my situation. I really do. But in my own defense, Jim's infatuation with Patricia from the advertising department at the newspaper where he works did not help matters much.

Ever since the start of summer he'd been talking about her. How stupid could he be? Did he not listen for even half a minute during his Psych 101 class? Did he really think that talking about her would somehow make his infatuation with her less transparent? Did he really think that I wanted to hear about her strong thigh muscles, muscles he's seen during their long runs together along the downtown Seattle piers at lunchtime?

And wasn't he making it clear as day that he had nothing at all nice to say about me?

Example:

What's her husband do again? I ask him one evening, after another too-long, too-descriptive, too transparently obsessive account of another oh-so-funny Patricia moment.

He's an idiot.

For a career?

He's a postman. Of all things.

What's wrong with being a postman? God, you'd think he was some kind of criminal or something.

I have half a mind to start talking about my co-worker Tom, who that very morning told me he liked my new haircut, something my husband has, as usual, failed to notice.

She deserves better than him, Jim says. It's not a good situation.

Me: I got my hair cut yesterday.

Jim (looking at my head like it's a rotting vegetable that he's discovered in the back of the refrigerator and that he's not positive he wants to touch): That's a haircut? You paid for that? They didn't even take anything off. Just waved the scissors over your head. What'd they charge for that, anyway?

A much longer example:

When I married Jim, I made him throw out the

boxloads of letters from old girlfriends he'd managed to collect over the years. To his credit, he took the boxes to the dump without argument and threw the lot of them in with the rest of the trash—his former universe, the evidence of his sexual conquests, nothing but a pile of garbage. For my part, I put my old love letters in a shoe box and hid them in the back of a drawer in the study, behind the photographs I've never managed to put into albums.

Every once in a while I pull out my shoe box of letters and take a brief vacation into my past life. The one I spent with Ray. This is what I'm doing a few weeks before Melissa and Greg's wedding—reading the old shit Ray wrote me from faraway places over the years—when who should call in the middle of my reminiscing but my ever-present husband, the one who isn't Ray, asking me if he should come by and pick me up, or if I'd rather just meet up with everybody at the restaurant.

There are good parts to being a terrible listener. Gwen can repeat herself over and over, for instance, and I won't realize that she's saying the same old boring thing she's said a million times before. Or when someone tells a joke—I immediately forget the punch line, and I can hear the same joke again the very next day and I'll laugh the same spontaneous laugh I laughed before.

The main drawback to this is the fact that I never seem to be able to hang on to the stuff I really ought to plaster my brain's bulletin board with. The important stuff. Like birthdays. Or yearly Pap smear appointments. Or when Steve at work told me that he had a sister who died in a plane crash, and I plumb forgot and made a really bad joke about his upcoming flight crashing. Things like that.

And I really should have remembered the going-away party for one of Jim's colleagues at the newspaper: six o'clock for cocktails, with dinner following. Damn. I really should have remembered to remember that one.

Whenever I'm feeling in a panic, I call Elsa. She is my one true friend at work, the one person to whom I can mention things from my life without obsessing for hours later over what she must think of me. Elsa. Of strong German stock. Eyes as blue-black as a bruise. Tall and blond, with legs up to her ears and big feet to match. You could see her in another life in a gingham apron, milking cows and baking batches of blueberry muffins. But Elsa prefers miniskirts and big funny brooches she creates herself, which adorn most of her outfits, making her a prime candidate for ultimate outsider at the school where we both ended up working. I'm a distant second in the shadow of Elsa's towering persona, something for which I will be eternally grateful.

Elsa has always shaved her pubic hair because, she says, her husband, Claude, likes her to look like a little girl. Anything I could tell Elsa about my own life would pale in comparison to her confessing to an itchy vulva.

I work part-time, which is a good thing. More than three days a week and I'd go crazy. The kids I can deal with. They are for the most part cute, except for the ones who are, honestly, not very cute, but instead obnoxious and smelly, which, I'm afraid, a good deal of them are. Yet even a smelly, obnoxious kid is a few floors above the sub-zero-basement mentality of the vast majority of teachers at the school. It's like a small, ugly miracle, the assortment of dumbshits in positions of authority. And I am among them, which I suppose is justice, considering that I'm a bit of a dumbshit myself.

Elsa, however, says I'm like a breath of fresh air in the dank atmosphere in which she works and breathes. I'm afraid a breath of fresh air for Elsa would still be contaminated with multiple toxins, but I'll take a compliment anywhere I can get one.

So now I call Elsa and tell her that I'm about to go to a party with Jim where the infamous Patricia will be present and that I need a pep talk to get me through the evening.

Maybe she'll get drunk and make a fool of herself, Elsa says.

With my luck, she looks fabulous drunk, I say.

Then let's hope she's a barfer.

I have nothing to wear to the dinner, which if I don't get a move on I may miss anyway, making the lack of appropriate clothing in my possession essentially a nonissue. Nonetheless, I search. You'd think there would be one complete outfit among the dozens of blouses and skirts and dresses and shoes that constitute the carnival inside my closet. Perhaps if I were a fashion editor for some stylish women's magazine, I'd be able to pull off a look consisting only of items bearing no relation to one another. Perhaps not. Why can I not own one single pair of decent shoes?

I finally yank a shapeless yet dependable little black dress from the rack and sniff at the armpits. Not horrible. It will have to do.

No heavy drinking tonight, I lecture my reflection in the mirror. But there is that sneaky face smirking back at me, as usual.

I am late. Jim doesn't even pretend to be happy to see me. Less than that: He doesn't even glance in my direction once he's done giving me that face of his, the one where for all intents and purposes he appears to be smiling when really he is pissed as all get-out. The antismile. Patricia is seated to his right, looking not a day over sixteen. She is a strawberry on the vine, unblemished, ripe for picking.

Brad, who works the sports desk with Jim, makes room for me, pulling up a chair from another table and calling out to the waiter for another wineglass. He is at least eight sheets to the wind at this point, Brad being a man who loves his wine more than just about anything, barring, I'm guessing, his penis. But that's just a guess. As much as he drinks, his penis couldn't possibly be useful anyway.

I sit down and Brad immediately hucks up next to me, shoulder to shoulder, and through a pair of eyes wet as a fish, asks where I've been.

You know us gals, I say, for lack of anything better.

No, Brad says. He lets out a phlegm-filled chortle. But I sure as hell wish I did!

Jim's been at the paper for nearly seventeen years. He has his own column, where he gets to comment on all those slivers of minutiae that sports fans find so fascinating. Sports as constant metaphor for life. Sports as lesson in manhood, in humanity, in character building or the lack of it. Jim loves nothing more than a sports figure whom he can call a "class act." He loves the life stories he reports on, the struggles and failures and the sometime successes that happen even when no one believed success possible. He's a good writer. His column is popular. At the top there's a postage stamp–sized picture of him from when he had more hair. If you knew him only from that one picture and a steady reading of his columns, you'd think he was an all-right guy. You'd probably imagine him playing a round of golf with buddies, shooting the breeze over a pitcher or two of beer. You'd probably think he was happily married, to a devoted wife, the love of his life. You'd probably think she loved him right back.

I finally shake Brad loose, or more factually, Brad finally shuts up and stares at the plate of food in front of him, as though trying to figure out exactly how to ingest a solid. His steak resembles a piece of dead meat, which, of course, it is. But a steak shouldn't look that way. A steak should bear no resemblance to the electrocuted, sliced-open cow it once was. I feel a bit sick seeing his plate myself.

In my moment of unexpected freedom, I glance across the table to find my husband entertaining Patricia with some clearly newly concocted story which, unbelievably, entails his saving the life of an unsuspecting Joe by pushing the guy out of the path of an out-of-control car a millisecond before impact. My husband the hero. Patricia looks impressed.

What is it that Patricia's got that I haven't got? Okay, so she's at least ten years younger, I'll give her that. And she's got legs up to her ears. Can't take that away from her. And she's got those kind of straight, sexy bangs that hang like a flimsy bathrobe over her big, unlined eyes.

But has she the wisdom of the years? Has she the wisdom of parenting? Of marriage? Of knowing what it's like to live with someone who insists on flossing his teeth, night after night, while sitting buck naked on the edge of the bed, watching *SportsCenter* while bits of used food shoot out toward the screen?

Well?

I watch my husband ask Patricia to dance. He walks her to the dance floor and they launch into a fake swing-dance thing, Jim whirling her around, his demeanor making it obvious that he knows that he doesn't know what he's doing. Patricia circles around him, her shiny hair bouncing around her shoulders like she's the star of a shampoo commercial. My husband has a big stupid grin, watching her.

Brad pokes me in the back.

Want to dance? he asks.

He is drenched in sweat from his previous forays onto the dance floor. His face shines like a waxy corpse.

Okay, I say.

We walk toward the dancing crowd, everybody loose by now. There is a lot of flailing of arms and twirling. The moment we reach the wooden square of the dance floor, the music switches to a slow number. Within seconds, things have cleared out—people return to their seats for a breather. Brad gives me no chance for escape. He reaches for me with damp hands and pulls me in close. I am nearly overcome with the smell of alcohol and sweat. I attempt to keep a few inches between us while Brad attempts to close the gap. Turning my head away from his shoulder and the undeniable stench of his armpit, I catch sight of Jim and Patricia, still dancing together. She has both hands wrapped around his neck, as she leans back to chat with him while their bodies nearly touch at their middles. I can't stand to watch them. I can't stand to see my husband so enamored with another woman. I consider waltzing over to the two of them and slapping him across the face. But then the song ends, and I disengage myself from Brad's clammy embrace and excuse myself for the ladies' room.

We've driven in separate cars, so we don't have to drive home together. This gives me a good fifteen minutes to compose myself. I pull up in front of the house and see that Jim has, as usual, beaten me home. It is one of his goals in life: to always beat me home. All the lights are on in the house. It looks like a spaceship about to take off.

I don't want to go in. I already know what awaits me inside. Silence. Followed by his outraged denials of outrageous flirtatiousness. That smile that isn't a smile. Who needs to hurry to see any of that?

I drive slowly down the block, wondering how the other people do it. The other people being all of my seemingly happy-go-lucky neighbors, the ones who drive in and out of their driveways, garage doors dropping electronically behind them like so many final curtains. Okay, so maybe Mrs. Wilkins gassed herself behind her garage door last year. And maybe the Gilders just separated, and maybe Kassie Jacobs let drop that she made a porno movie for a little extra cash in college, but basically they all seem—tonight anyway—to be living their quiet, happy lives behind their quiet, happy closed curtains. Everybody in the world, so damn happy.

I pull over in front of a dark house a couple of blocks down and sit for a while, wondering how terrible it would be if I sped off to California and knocked on Ray's door. Picturing Ray waiting on his front porch (does he have a front porch?), asking me, What took you so long?

5

Relationship Test #2:

Josh and Sally are engaged. Even though it goes against their modern-day, who-gives-a-shit-what-the-plates-look-like, why-are-we-bothering grain, they finally acquiesce to convention and agree to register for kitchen items at Bloomingdale's. A Saturday is put aside to accomplish this archaic task. Things grow difficult when they find they cannot agree on a pattern for their dishes. Josh wants something traditional, something reminiscent of the platters and plates his grandmother used to set out for family gatherings. Sally wishes for something with a contemporary look, is intrigued by the Asian-influenced plates that to Josh hardly resemble plates at all, but look more like giant square ashtrays. There, in the heart of the housewares department at Bloomingdale's, they begin to bicker, Sally wondering when in the world it became the husband's business what fucking pattern is picked for the registry, Josh replying that he had no idea his wife still considered such old-fashioned sexist notions palatable.

You advise the engaged couple to:

A. Break up immediately.

B. Agree on a pattern that neither of them particularly likes but that neither finds particularly objectionable either, with the knowledge that for the rest of their married lives together they will have to eat off the same unliked yet nonobjectionable plates every single day, and will thereby be constantly reminded of the ominous fight they once had in the housewares department of Bloomingdale's, back when there was still time to call the whole thing off before they were stuck once and for all not only with the plates but with each other.

A few days after Melissa and Greg's wedding, Jim decides, out of the blue, that the two of us should go away for the weekend. He says this as though it were a perfectly normal thing to say. As if we were a perfectly normal, fun-loving couple who plans things like weekends away as a matter of course. As if we did it all the time instead of never.

I think, he says, that we ought to go somewhere this weekend.

For a moment, I do not speak. I try to mentally pry out the source of this suggestion. Why now? Why the sudden show of attention? He couldn't possibly be merely and sincerely asking his wife to go away with him for a weekend, could he?

I mean, he says that we ought to get away. Really. Do something fun together for a change.

I ignore the obvious implication of this statement— that we are the no-fun couple—in order to focus my concentration on ignoring the guilt-inducing fun I'd had only last weekend with Ray. In fact, I'm unable to ignore any of it.

You don't have to work this weekend? I ask.

Nah, he says.

No big games to cover? No recently arrested athletes? No recruiting scandals?

God, Julia. Stop. Can't a guy want to go away with his wife?

A momentary personal earthquake shakes my brain, like an omen from God. But what, exactly, is the message? Thoughts crash from their shelves and shatter across the floor. In the ensuing mayhem, I find myself giving Jim a thumbs-up to the weekend.

* * *

At least one day a week, Elsa and I eat lunch at the diner around the corner, mostly because we know no one else from Edison would ever eat there. The place has a not-so-out-of-line reputation for filth and smoke—two things that don't bother the two of us. The place isn't all that filthy, really. No bugs crawling on the walls, no apparent attempts to rearrange old food on new plates and pass it off as fresh. Largely only the illusion of filth, helped along by the deficient lighting and the more than occasional lipstick-stained mug. But given that Elsa and I have been on diets for at least the last decade, we have grown to appreciate the diner's peculiarly appetite-squelching charms.

Today I am feeling guilty. So over a plate of oil-soaked fries and a Diet Coke without the lemon that I always ask for but that is never brought, no matter how many times I ask for a Diet Coke with lemon, I let the cat out of the bag and ask Elsa if she thinks it's okay for me to have slept with a man who is not my husband.

Elsa doesn't hesitate for a second. She lives to be asked this type of question.

Honey, she says. You only live once.

As always, I leave a huge tip.

* * *

My sister Stacy has always liked Jim, probably because he flirts with her incessantly and she's just dumb enough not to see that he pulls that number on anything with a vagina. You can actually witness her droopy-flower body perk up a few notches whenever she enters a room and finds the fountain of Jim inside.

Stacy's own husband, Paul, is a fat man. He's not just big, or large, or portly. He's fat. That's simply a statement of fact. And she married him fat, which, I suppose, means she fell in love with his mind instead of his body, although the fact that he's also rich may have had something to do with it.

Stacy and I are not close, but about once a month we force a sisterly bond by chatting on the phone for a few minutes. We talk about our husbands, our hair, our newest purchases, but mainly we talk about our mother. It's one of those human conundrums—the fact that the one person we least want to think about is the exact same person we find the most easy to discuss. She is the source of our most concrete bond.

Anyway, Stacy and the fat man offer to have Chad over for the weekend while Jim and I are away.

We'd love to have him, Stacy says.

And even though he's fifteen years old and has more or less been on his own for the last few years, and even though no self-respecting fifteen-year-old would ever consent to having others look after him in the absence of his parents, and even though he'll never speak to me again if I take my sister up on the offer, and even though I know the chances of Chad's actually showing up at Stacy's house are exceedingly slim if not impossible, I say, That would be great, he'll be there on Friday. He's pretty much sworn off speaking to me throughout eternity anyway. Won't make much difference if he tacks on a few more days.

The Oregon coast. That's where Jim takes me. In November. Have you ever been to the Oregon coast in November? Of course not. And that's because you know better than to think a walk on the beach in November in the most freezing corner of the universe is a good idea. No one in his right mind goes to the Oregon coast in November. No one, period, goes to the Oregon coast in November. The place is empty. The place is barren, stripped, vacant. One never-ending moonscape of sand running parallel to one huge, dark, eerie expanse of ocean. Tens of sleepy little shops hunkered down, numbly depressing in their whitewashed emptiness. To this utterly bottomless vacuum of a black hole, Jim brings me, with sex on his brain. And since there is nothing else to do in this town except stare out the window and seek to discern the faint demarcation line between water and sky in the limitless distance, I decide what the hell, and fuck my husband.

I once watched an entire episode of *I Love Lucy* while some poor jerk lay on top of me, pumping away in his own quiet world of desperation. He might as well have not been there. That's not exactly how it is to have sex with Jim after a dry spell of a couple of months. Still, on a scale of 1 to 10 with 1 being watching *I Love Lucy* while fucking and 10 being losing myself in a sea of ecstasy, I'd have to give our afternoon in the hotel room in Oregon about a 2. Not that Jim isn't good in bed. He's quite good, actually. Especially when you take into account the fact that he's most often up against a corpselike wife. No, the reason I'd have to give the entire afternoon of multiple couplings a 2 is that I had Ray on the brain the whole time, and not in the "Imagine this is Ray instead of Jim" kind of on-the-brain, but the "I'm so depressed right now without Ray" kind of on-the-brain. Making it difficult to concentrate.

Some of the things I've been asked to do over the years by various men in my life: Fuck a banana. Fuck his best friend. Fuck his best friend and him at the same time. Fuck during a movie. Fuck in the men's rest room of a restaurant. Fuck in the bathroom of his parents' house. Beat him off under the table. Beat him off in his car while he's driving. Suck his dick at the movies, a restaurant, a park, a museum, in an alley, on the front lawn, behind the Taco Bell, on the beach, in the bathtub, in the ocean, on the back deck, in a closet, in a tent, on a picnic table, on a kitchen table, under the kitchen table, on a sheepskin rug, in a hallway, in a public swimming pool, in various hot tubs, in cars, buses, trains, airplanes, on hikes, on walks, while reading, while eating, while sleeping, while showering, while sitting, while gardening, while cooking, while emptying the dishwasher, while sweeping the floor, while playing the piano, while paying bills, while cleaning out my wallet, while doing the laundry, while making the bed, while talking on the telephone, while opening a bottle of wine, while sweating, while bike riding, while simply moving through space, while doing nothing discernible at all except wondering if he is about to ask me to suck his dick.

Jim, fortunately, does not ask me to suck his dick while we're in Oregon.

Question:
Do all men use their penises as flag stands? Do they all

find hanging towels or dishcloths or underwear or socks or ties over their erect penises to be hilarious? Because in my experience, this is what men do. If there is one man out there in the universe who has never done such a thing—be honest—I'd like to know about it.

In a stroke of good luck, *Planes, Trains and Automobiles* is playing on television and Jim surprises me by agreeing to watch it instead of some football game I know he's been dying to watch. I can't help wondering what's gotten into my husband, what with the weekend away and the offer to miss a football game, but I don't examine the matter too closely. Nothing ever stays the same for too long in this crazy thing called my marriage, so I decide to just play it as it lays and not ruin things by talking about them. Sometimes a breakdown in communication is the only viable option.

Jim makes a pile out of the pillows at the head of the hotel bed and we both lean back against them to watch the movie, just the way I've always imagined old happily married couples do. At the foot of the bed, our four sets of toes stick up into the air like miniature people who've come to watch the movie with us. There's something funny about our four sets of toes, and finally I realize that the funny thing is that Jim's toes are not in the least recognizable to me. I am not at all familiar with Jim's toes, with

Jim's feet. They are strangers to me, those ten little pink piggies with a small garden of black hairs sprouting from the two big toes. Utter strangers. And this fact—that I do not know my own husband's feet; that I would not be able to pick his toes out from a lineup, if ever necessary; that his toes look strange and new in their unique bumpy existences—drains me of all energy, leaves me unable to enjoy Steve Martin and John Candy, a state of mind unheard of until that moment.

Just as I expected, Chad never makes it to Stacy and Paul's. Poor Stacy leaves a series of panic-stricken phone messages on my answering machine, telling Chad to call her as soon as he gets this message because she's worried about him and responsible for him and, besides, it's kind of rude to not show up when you're supposed to and not even call to give a heads-up, and she's not sure what to do now, should she call the police, and would he please please please give her a call immediately, and so on and so forth until the tape fills up.

And no messages waiting for me from Ray, either. Of course, he doesn't call. Of course, he returns to his southern California life without so much as a glance back. Of course, he doesn't send me flowers or a card or a goofy joke present and he doesn't leave vaguely sexy messages on my voice mail at work and he doesn't even take the two seconds it would take to leave me an e-mail saying how nice it was to see me, much less fuck me. No, Ray just leaves as Ray always does, and I'm still here, same as ever.

I decide never to speak to him again. This seems to be the most sane advice I have ever prescribed to myself, and I am shocked to have not thought of it sooner. No speaking to Ray. No letting him creep into my head at all hours. No letting him live out his California life in my brain while I stand under the shower head until the water turns cold. No more late-night silent phone calls. No more checking my e-mails and finding nothing there. A clean break. A blank slate. An empty heart, all of the old junky love feelings taken to the dump and tossed onto the garbage heap. Today, I tell myself, I am a new person, a new woman. Today is the first day of the rest of my Ray-free life.

Two Klonopins ought to get me through the first couple of hours.

On the Monday after our weekend together, Jim continues his string of surprising moves by coming home from work

in time for dinner. Too bad I haven't prepared anything.
In my own defense, it's not as though he'd made it home
any earlier than nine o'clock for weeks on end.

What are you doing home so early? I ask.

Excuse me?

You. Home. Early. What's going on?

Nothing, really. Just done at the office for the day.

He goes upstairs to change, comes down a few minutes later in running clothes. He's way too fit these days.
Way too many lunches spent running with Patricia.

You didn't run at lunch today? I ask.

No.

You made poor Patricia run alone?

Jim leans against the wall to stretch one of his calves.
He doesn't look in my direction.

She wasn't around today, he says.

Sick?

No, he says. Not sick.

Okay. Not sick. Fired?

No. Not fired.

Okay. Not sick. Not fired. What is it? She die over the
weekend? Get hit by a truck? Fall into a coma?

Not funny, Jim says. She went away for the weekend
with her husband.

Jim's face tightens. It's the look someone makes after
a major toe-stubbing. It's painfully obvious that our little

sojourn to Cannon Beach was nothing more than a little tit to Patricia's tat.

And apparently they decided to stay an extra day, he says.

Well! I say. What a wild and crazy postman she married!

6

After the Oregon trip, I'm in no mood to work. I'd like to be able to say that my lack of motivation is unusual. In truth, the fact that I am expected to actually perform some sort of work when I show up at work is one of those things I've never been able to come to grips with. Not that I'm lazy. It's just that there are so many things to take care of before any real work can begin. For one, I must buy a cup of coffee from Roger at the corner hardware shop, where "the coffee's always on!" and put up with the daily few minutes of chatter which must be put up with when purchasing coffee from Roger at the corner hardware shop. And then I must pick up the morning newspaper from the newspaper box outside the drugstore, which often entails entering the drugstore to buy something small like a pack of gum in order to have change to buy the newspaper (because God forbid they should ever consider giving you change for a dollar without any purchase at all). After buying coffee and the newspaper, I must then, of course, consume both in the privacy of the space that is formally called the "resource room," but that I refer to as my office. And with good reason, seeing as how I have taken up for my personal use all the resources the room has to offer. Which isn't much, only a desk, and a round table with chairs, and a few shelves of books and materials that haven't been used since my first day in the resource room, which was, I hate to admit, more than twelve years ago. Twelve years in the resource room. Not very resourceful of me.

The kids I work with, however, are a resourceful lot. They know not to disturb the resource room para-professional with dumb questions if the resource room para-professional is busy drinking her coffee and reading her newspaper. This all-important rule is one of the earliest drilled into their little heads when first confronted with resource room etiquette. And I believe that the lack of learning of rules and sticking to them is what landed half these kids in the resource room to begin with. That and the fact that they can't read. So I am role-modeling for them, also an important factor in any para-professional role. I am role-modeling the enjoyment one can get from reading the newspaper without interruption. I am role-modeling quiet time and resourcefulness.

Some of the kids are so resourceful once they learn the rules of the resource room that they don't bother showing up at all. I applaud their willingness to look in new directions, such as the girls' rest room or out back behind the play structure. I applaud their ability to take what's thrown at them and toss it back, a skill best learned while still young.

An additional technique I have skillfully employed over the years to assist me in making it through the work day is the ever-helpful distraction of a crush. At times, finding someone appropriate to bestow a crush on can be difficult, as I learned when I had to settle on the fish guy behind the counter at the supermarket, or when I decided the man who checks the water-meter readings really wasn't all that bad-looking if you could get beyond the sweaty armpits. Crushes foil the boredom. All of which is only a lame attempt to explain the fact of my embarrassing schoolgirl crush on Tom at work. I'm not positive what brings it about, although it may have something to do with the fact that Tom is cute and his jeans do that thing where they hang just right off his hips, and also that he works with the severely screwed-up students and doesn't seem to mind getting told by smart-ass kids that he needs a haircut when, in fact, he is nearly bald. This baldness thing he has going is weirdly attractive. Not in a cool-guy Kojak way, or a regal Yul Brynner way, or even in an I'm-way-too-cool-to-care way. No, Tom's baldness is more like a sensitive guy's sensitive-guy way. Like he's so unperturbed by his lack of hair that he's got room to ponder someone else's troubles. Which, for a guy, is pretty amazing, if you think about it.

Tom started it, I suppose, by being so utterly himself, which is to say, so utterly the opposite of Jim. It's probably not a good thing that I give Tom brownie points every time he says or does something that Jim would never think of saying or doing. For instance, I'm quite certain that Tom would never consider taking a trip to the Oregon coast in November. It would probably be better if I could just appreciate Tom for who he is instead of for being the anti-Jim. But that's the way it goes. It's better than those dry spells when I've got no one to have a decent crush on. Besides, it's not like I'm going to tell Tom I'm dying to sleep with him or anything.

First rule of crushes: Never admit your crush to your crush.

But I do admit my crush to Gwen. She is drinking iced tea from a giant frosted glass. As always, she offers me some. As always, I say no.

I tell her, It's reached that point where I'm afraid to look at him because I might turn red.

You know what I have to say to that, Gwen says.

And I do know what she has to say, because it's the same thing she says about everything—that if you keep looking in other places for certain things, then the true answer to your search is probably staring you in the face in your own backyard. Gwen's *Wizard of Oz* Theory of Life, which is one of the two things I find truly annoying about her—the fact that *The Wizard of Oz* plays such a major-league role in her view of the world.

Gwen's living room is pathologically clean. I watch as she plucks at a stray bit of thread invading the freshly vacuumed carpet. She's just had fake fingernails glued to her own chewed-up ones, so she has to take several swipes at the thread with the pads of her fingertips before successfully retrieving it. She sets it gingerly in the palm of her other hand and holds it there, aloft.

There's nothing in my backyard but dog shit, I tell her.

The other truly annoying thing about Gwen is the fact that she has a mother whom she genuinely likes and who does things like drop by and then immediately leave when she senses that her timing for a visit isn't quite working out. Every single facet of that last sentence is so far from my own experience with my mother that it may as well be something I read about in *National Geographic*, right next to the picture of a Pygmy tribesman holding a dead, bulge-eyed unidentifiable animal in his fist. Further, actually.

My own mother is nothing like Gwen's mother. My own mother would delight in arriving at my house unexpectedly and finding that she has come at the worst possible time. The joy she takes from her daughter's housewife hardships is directly proportional to the horror I take in her discoveries of same. You'd think there'd be one ounce of compassion locked inside her somewhere. You'd think every human being, in order to be labeled "human," would have to have at least one single cell of humanity floating amid the billions upon billions of other cells that somehow, miraculously, cluster together in our mutually exclusive yet undeniably similar humanoid shapes. But no. My mother is lacking something crucial on that cellular level.

As Gwen would say, If she only had a heart.

My mother: So where is Chad?

Me: I don't know.

My mother: What do you mean, you don't know?

Me: I mean, I don't know where he is right now, is what I mean.

My mother: Well, why don't you know? A grandmother comes to visit and her grandson's not here and his own mother doesn't know where he is? I don't understand it.

Me: What part don't you understand?

My mother: Are you playing with me?

Me: Excuse me?

My mother: Because I don't like it. I'll tell you that right now. It's not nice. A daughter to play with her mother that way. No wonder Chad isn't here. No wonder he doesn't want to be around you. Playing that way as if it was funny. Well, ha ha. Big comedienne. Very funny woman you turned out to be.

Me: You lost me.

My mother: What do you mean by that?

Me: I mean, you lost me somewhere in there with all of the you're-so-funny-I-forgot-to-laugh whatever-it-is you're talking about.

My mother: Are you playing with me?

Chad, as it turns out, is at his girlfriend's house, making out in her bedroom. I know this because Chad's girlfriend's mother calls to tell me that Chad is a bad influence on her little Tricia, that Chad very well knows Tricia's mother's rules about closed bedroom doors and that she thinks I, as Chad's mother, ought to be doing some very heavy-duty talking about sexually communicated diseases and pregnancy before one thing leads to another, if I know what she means.

Mothering is everything it's cracked up to be, which is to say, a complete and total nightmare. Anyone who tells you differently is not to be trusted.

Among the many brilliant teaching techniques I have learned to implement in order to bring out the best in my students, is my Word of the Day. Each morning, on the board in the front of the room, I write a new and fascinating Word of the Day, followed by a brilliantly constructed sentence using that word. I do this for two reasons. One, it helps to quell the boredom, knowing that I've got my *Random House Dictionary of the English Language* to look forward to, knowing that I can waste a good half-hour searching for just the right new vocabulary word to get all of us through the day, knowing that I'll have a chance to enjoy that chalky feeling on my fingers that I imagine real teachers must enjoy as they energetically throw math equations or deep philosophical thoughts up on the board. And two, who knows? Maybe one day some of the resource room kids will at last glance up from their CD players or the games on their cell phones, or their latest issues of *Vogue* or *InStyle* or *Maxim* or *Skateboarding* or *Rolling Stone*, and find they have actually learned something, if only a new vocabulary word, from their glance up at the board. Hasn't happened yet, but I can always hold out hope.

Today I use the method of choice for days when a half-hour browse through the *Random House Dictionary of the English Language* isn't going to do it for me. I use the open-and-point method. I flip through the pages at random and stop whenever my subconscious instructs, then set a finger on the page. Voilà.

"Moxie," I write. "Sometimes it takes moxie to get up in the morning."

Even though I do not take advice from others easily, if at all, I have to admit that Tricia's mother may have a point. How to go about it, though? I haven't discussed sex with Chad since he grew old enough to have any idea what I was talking about. My theory on presenting the facts of life was to pour out all the uncomfortable information long before adolescence and then let it sink in over the course of several years. After that, I handed the bat over to Jim, who altogether failed to step up to the plate.

I wait until Chad gets up late one Sunday morning and then, in the most normal tone I can summon, I offer him pancakes.

Why? he asks.

Must there be a reason? I say. Can't a mother make her son pancakes?

Chad's hair looks like a bad wig, all matted and shoved out of place. I love him like this. I love first-thing-in-the-morning Chad, with his matted hair and bad breath. I reach into the fridge and pull out a bottle of the expensive organic orange juice I recently bought while under the influence of one of my infrequent health kicks. I'm already regretting the lettuce, which will take me hours to free of gritty sand and tiny gray slugs. Between gray slugs and chemicals, I'll take the chemicals.

Want some? I ask. I shake the bottle. I unscrew the cap. I make detours and shortcuts through my brain, searching for an appropriately cute yet serious way to start talking about what I think we ought to be talking about. I don't come up with anything suitable. I hold the bottle far enough away from my face to scrutinize the label's list of organic contents. Next thing you know, the uncapped bottle has slipped from between my fingers. Chad reaches out in a heroic effort to make a save, but it's too late. The bottle twirls, flips, and drops to the floor. In a miracle of nature or God or just plain freakdom, it lands lip-edge down, unbroken. None of the juice spills.

Chad and I both stare at the bottle. It looks so innocent, upside down on the floor like that, acting as though bottles pulled off this nifty trick all the time. But Chad and I both know better. We have just witnessed what will from here on out be referred to as the Miracle of the Organic Orange Juice Bottle.

Unbelievable, Chad says.

We spend the next few minutes looking and laughing and devising ways to pick up the bottle without making the expensive organic orange juice spill onto the floor. Chad takes a few pictures for posterity. Finally he makes a mad grab for the bottle and turns it upright. Only a tiny orange puddle remains behind.

Chad gives me the old slant-eye, which I immediately recognize as my hereditary gift to him.

Sit, he says to me. I'll make the pancakes.

And I do. I sit and eat Chad's pancakes, all the while telepathically delivering an articulate treatise on the merits of safe sex. Afterward, I do the dishes.

7

I tell my therapist all about Ray and the wedding and Jim and the Oregon coast, and then I think about quitting my therapist altogether. What good is he? Shouldn't I have gotten a grip by now? After paying hundreds and hundreds and hundreds of dollars to talk to this man, shouldn't I have seen at least a slight movement toward progress? I never expected to see an entire mountain of change, but shouldn't I have gotten a small hill by now? A mound? A pimple's worth?

And yet here we are, week after week, going over the same goddamn things: Ray. Jim. Ray. Chad. Ray. My mother. Ray. It's humiliating.

Maybe I'm missing something. Maybe the process in-
volves boring myself so thoroughly with the facts of my
own life that I at last do something to change things.
Maybe there's a world of advice in my therapist's shrugs.

By the time Thanksgiving break arrives, I'm exhausted.
You'd think it would occur to me that my exhaustion is
more intense than usual. You'd think it would occur to me
that this feeling-slightly-ill-in-the-morning business is
also more intense than usual. You'd think I'd put two and
two together and slap my forehead in the realization that
I've got a brand-new bun in the oven. But I don't. My
brain is occupied with depression.

The rain doesn't help. Have I mentioned that it rains
out here every single day? Nothing but gray upon gray
upon gray. Water, concrete, sidewalk, sky. All of it dull
and gray and depressing as a dirty ashtray. Chad once told
me an interesting fact, which is that really there is no such
thing as color, but that everything you look at is simply
white until your eyes do some miraculous thing with light,
leading you to believe that a leaf is green or a rose is red,
or that a mole on your back is still only brown and not yet
black or peculiarly shaped around the edges, which
would, of course, mean skin cancer. It's all in the lighting.
Which is why the entire world in this corner of the uni-

verse is gray. Because light can't find its way through the dense thicket of clouds that consistently loom overhead like the too-low ceilings of a cheap apartment.

That's your science fact for today.

So naturally, it is raining on Thanksgiving when we are due at four o'clock at Jim's parents' house for turkey and frozen peas and potatoes mashed with cubes and cubes of butter. It's raining really, really hard, and the freeways are packed with people all dressed up, holding candied yams in their laps, or bottles of wine, or pumpkin pies. Jim has made two loaves of zucchini bread, Chad a fruit salad, and I'm bringing up the rear with two bottles of white wine, a six-pack of Heinekens for Jim's dad, and a single thin joint that Elsa pressed into my palm on Wednesday after school, which I have checked for in my handbag three times since leaving the house.

There is an accident ahead on the freeway and we are forced into a single slow lane, windshield wipers working at hyperspeed, leaving momentary all-clear views of the car bumper in front of us, where a sticker continues to read: "Kick Ass." I wonder what compels people to put such a message on the back of their car, and then I wonder what, exactly, the message means, and then I wonder at what point did it become acceptable in our society to use the word "ass" so blatantly and openly, and finally I realize that I've most likely spent at least ten times longer considering the "Kick Ass" bumper sticker than the asshole who put it on his car did in the first place. And then I want to kick his ass.

But the real story is that we drive past the car accident and it is a very sorry scene. A huge truck trailer on its side and two metal sculptures that were, until very recently, sedans or station wagons on their way to Grandma's or Aunt Tessa's and that are now scary reminders of the precariousness of life. And the thing about all of this is that I find myself wishing in that moment that it were me inside one of those smashed-up vehicles. Me on the way to the hospital with some caring technicians lovingly sticking tubes in my arms or an oxygen mask over my face. Me on my new road of helpless victim instead of on the freeway to Jim's parents' house. Which should give you some idea of how little I am looking forward to the evening.

Other People's Thanksgiving Plans:

Elsa is going to refuse to rent any more porno flicks for her husband over the long weekend. If he wants to watch porno, he's going to have to get his hand off his dick and go rent them himself.

Tom is flying to Pittsburgh to spend a perfectly normal Thanksgiving weekend with his perfectly normal family. I've asked him to bring a picture to show me, which was partly flirtatiousness and partly a perfectly normal, healthy curiosity about the baldness patterns running through his family. After all, if someday I'm going to have his child, I'd like to be fully informed.

Gwen and her husband are driving to California to see her sister. They will stop for lattes and cinnamon rolls and magazines, and no one will complain about wasting money on these items.

Ray. I don't know what Ray will be doing, so I can only torture myself with the possibilities which involve for the most part his seducing perfectly bodacious women in perfectly pristine beachlike environs, after imbibing perfectly prepared alcohol-soaked fruity drinks and dancing barefoot under one of those high, clear skies that my whole life I've been told exist somewhere out there in the universe.

My mother will spend Thanksgiving day at my sister Stacy's, complaining about me.

By the time we get to Jim's parents' house, I am a melancholy mess. Why is it that everything in life makes me think of Ray? Rain. Ray. Trees. Ray. Car wreck. Ray. It's just one never-ending, well-worn circular pathway in my brain.

Jim's dad opens the door. He is very happy to see us. That's what he says. I'm very happy to see you. Never have words sounded so insincere in the history of insincerity. Although he's definitely jazzed at the sight of the

Heineken six-pack I jangle from my index finger. Men are so easy to please.

It's a modern house, with sleek built-in window seats and bookcases, and low white furniture. The great expanse of white carpeting, unblemished, always gives me a chill. Where are the spills? The stains? The obvious traffic patterns through the plushness? It's as though no one actually lives here. The kitchen is a stainless-steel nightmare, all silver and glare. Somewhere a refrigerator door hides among the matching cabinets. God forbid there should be anything more than a perfect bowl of fruit on the countertop. God forbid anyone should see a toaster. And the bathrooms. Does anyone dare wet the shell-shaped soaps? The lace-trimmed white handtowels folded in matching exact rectangles? Would someone faint and hit his head on the gleaming white tile if a tissue somehow miraculously appeared in the bottom of the garbage basket next to the shining toilet?

Jim's mom falls against her son in cascading hellos. She is wearing a hideously flowered apron over an all-beige getup, her throat encased in fat fake pearls. A dozen bobby-pinned ringlets hang about her overly made-up face, an effect that leaves her resembling a scarily ancient little girl. She's obviously moved the cocktail hour up by a good half-day. She can barely get out one full, short sentence through all her slurry smiling.

Sorry we're late, Jim says. Accident on the freeway.

Oh, that's turrible, Jim's mom says. Turrible, terribly, turribly. Turrible.

Yeah, Jim says, and goes to make himself a drink.

The Jim Family Factlets:

Sister Diane. Married her high school sweetheart, tried everything to get pregnant, finally hired a surrogate mother to carry an implanted ovum created by Diane and her husband and a technician in Tucson. World's most expensive child was born with a mean case of colic and a big red cherry stain on her forehead, which all family members have pledged under threat of death to pretend not to see. Strident vegetarian. Strident about most things, actually.

Sister Tina. Baby of the family. A bit of a slut, if truth be known. But because she's the baby, everybody loves her.

Brother-in-law Ted. Married to Diane. Humorless, annoying environmental advocate. The type who makes you want to drink your coffee only in Styrofoam cups, or tell your kids to go ahead and throw their Popsicle sticks out the car window. Unfortunately, very good-looking in that careless, just-out-of-bed-hair way that no one but the truly good-looking can get away with. For some incomprehensible reason, adores Diane.

Jim.

Jim's dad, Wilson. Former accounting executive. Big

ears. Big blank space between his big ears. Big dumb attachment to all things golf-related. Thinks Jim could have done better in the wife department.

Jim's mom, Alice. The family spittoon.

Dinner goes fairly smoothly. No one touches the fake-turkey soy loaf that Diane has so thoughtfully prepared, as she does year after year. The Heinekens rapidly disappear, replaced by numerous bottles of expensive imported beers that at all times fill the cavernous extra refrigerator that Wilson keeps in the garage. Ted, who has piled his plate high with turkey breast and gravy despite his wife's sneering disapproval, amuses us with tales of recent environmental disasters and presidential misconduct. It's the yearly plot to goad big Wilson into a shouting match. This year, to my relief, it fails. Wilson valiantly ignores his son-in-law and busies himself making sure that everyone's glass stays full. I have to remind him three times that Chad is not old enough to drink alcohol before I finally give up and allow my son a beer, which he sucks down like a glass of chocolate milk.

It's when we get to Jim's zucchini bread, along with fruit cocktail embalmed in green Jell-O, and a pair of slightly burnt pumpkin pies, that Tina announces she has an announcement she'd like to make. This is long after

Chad has disappeared into the bowels of the rambling house to watch something inappropriate on one of the one hundred fifty-two channels Jim's parents pick up on their television set. But it's still early enough that Alice hasn't yet departed for the living room couch to nod off for the evening. So Tina's timing isn't too bad.

Tell, tell, Wilson says.

Brian and I are getting married, Tina says.

We all turn to look at the man-child sitting to Tina's left and as a group struggle to remember if this specimen is, indeed, Brian.

This guy? Wilson says.

Yes, Dad. This guy. Tina ruffles Brian's head of hair, which is a difficult task, given that Brian—an unusually short, unusually young, undeniably black-skinned man— has a tightly shorn afro. His tiny dark ears turn even darker at the tableful of scrutiny he's receiving, now that permission to stare at the only black person in the neighborhood has been granted.

You two? Wilson says.

Yes, Dad. Us two. Next June.

Wilson has a sudden need to clear his throat of some great impediment to his lungs. He makes two or three fantastic thrusting attempts and then gives up.

Well, God damn, he says, through a wall of phlegm. Welcome to the family, Brian.

There isn't a whole hell of a lot to do after that except

try to act as normal as possible. It isn't so much the fact that Tina is marrying a black person that's got everyone acting even more uncomfortable than the intensely uncomfortable way this family usually interacts. It's more that Tina is getting married at all. Tina, the embodiment of all things single, the shining example of how permissive parenting is one of the era's biggest errors in judgment, the girl who nearly brought down an entire senior class with genital herpes simplex complex—that Tina. Married. It's all a bit overwhelming.

Not to mention she's marrying a black man.

Alice, bless her heart, breaks open the champagne.

To marriage, she says, her voice quavering with emotion.

To marriage, we all repeat, or at least I think we all repeat it. Come to think of it, I'm not at all positive that Jim chimed in.

I momentarily consider asking Chad to share Elsa's joint in the downstairs bathroom. It seems to me about time we both fess up to being pot smokers instead of keeping up this façade of Cleaverville. But I decide against it. Wise parenting choice, seeing as how, as it happens, he's already swiped it from my purse.

As I stand alone in the downstairs bathroom, jointless,

a depressing thought hits me. Without my being aware of it, the very last time I picked up Chad came and went. I wonder how old he was. I wonder what the reason for picking him up could have been, why it was that I leaned over to grab him beneath his smooth, pink armpits and then raised him to my chest, probably saying something dumb like, You're getting too big for Mommy! Because he would have been long and lanky by then. He'd have been, what?—ten? eleven? No longer the little boy I used to smother with kisses, set on the bed to tickle his sweet tummy with my forehead. No longer the baby with the full, throaty laugh, more real than anything I'd ever heard in my life. No longer the boy who liked to set his little hand against my cheek, turn my face toward his. Days on end, we'd sit, just the two of us, maybe the television on, maybe Mister Rogers tossing his sneaker from one hand to the other, welcoming Mister McFeely to the neighborhood. Or Chad asleep in my arms, his warm, perfect body making me weepy for all of the dead babies in the Holocaust while I stared at the top of his lovely head, at the two wondrous cowlicks set down right next to each other, two amazing spirals of black hair, so silky and fine and smelling exactly like the word *fresh*.

That time came and went. I picked him up and set him down and then he was too big and I never did it again.

Nothing to do now but study my face in the mirror. God, I look old. Old, old, old. I turn off the bathroom light to see if a change in lighting might help. No such luck.

Circular thoughts attack me: The happiness on Tina's face. My inability to be big enough to be happy for her when I am so unhappy. My husband's obvious unhappiness. The growing distance between Chad and me. My being unhappy when I have a life that others would die for. My unhappiness at my current self-consciousness in allowing myself five minutes of self-centered misery when the world is a fucked-up place and people keep dying or killing each other, or living in lonely despair, everywhere. My own stupid wedding day and the wedding day I didn't have, the one where I am marrying Ray and he is happy to be marrying me and we are happy to be together and everyone is happy for us. And then back to happy Tina and chastising myself for not enjoying her moment of happiness and telling myself that as soon as I finish scrutinizing my wrinkles I will go upstairs and tell everyone how goddamn happy I am. Happy. Happy. Happy.

I turn the light back on and give myself the old slant-eye in the mirror.

Happy Thanksgiving, I say.

* * *

I emerge from the bathroom to find Tina and Brian gone, off to inform Brian's family of their good news, leaving the rest of us to discuss them openly in their absence.

Wilson begins. He seems like a very nice boy, he says.

We all agree.

He's a lawyer, Diane adds.

Lots of head nodding.

Well, I think it's just great, Ted says.

More head nodding.

Alice begins to sob.

Mother, Diane says. It's the twenty-first century. Get over it.

That's not it, Alice says. She pokes at her eyes with a beige handkerchief, smearing her mascara further. Her cheeks are bright fuchsia balls.

A lawyer! she croaks between sobbing breaths. My Tina's marrying a lawyer!

8

Relationship Test #3:

You have been married five years. One day, a package arrives in the mail. It is addressed to you. You can't tell who has sent it, or where it was sent from. It is a mystery. You love mysteries. The package holds something mysteriously wonderful. You need scissors to open the box. You cut at the tape carefully so as not to damage the mysterious contents. Something is wrapped in brown paper inside. You smile to yourself. This is fun. You pick up the brown wrapped thing. It has the shape of a book. But no. It is too light to be a book. You laugh a little, lightly. There is a card taped to the brown paper that wraps the booklike mysterious object. You open the card. It is from your husband. "For my wife, with love," it says. You laugh, loudly this time. You turn the package over, wedge your index finger under the tape that binds the paper together, and tear it loose. The paper falls away. You stare down into your lap. It is a video—Part One of a series. *The Guide to Better Sex*.

Choose from the following:

A. This is a good gift.

B. This is a lousy gift.

C. This isn't a gift at all.

Monday morning, five kids are struggling over the same assignment from their English class. It seems simple enough. A one-page essay, no spelling errors, on the theme "My Perfect Saturday." It seems the kind of assignment that ought to take five minutes, max. But this is the resource room. This is the place for mostly bright, yet thoroughly unmotivated students to live out their unmotivated school days. And so instead of buckling down and giving "My Perfect Saturday" the five minutes it deserves, there is much complaining and shrugging and claiming of sleepiness and long weekends. Then there is trouble finding something to write with and paper that is not wide-ruled and the problem of someone's having to use the bathroom and then everyone else's suddenly having to use the bathroom as well. After everybody finally returns from the bathroom, there are requests to open the window, to close the window, to listen to music, to get a drink of water, and to tell Jonathan to shut up.

Okay, I say. If everybody will give it the old college try for just five minutes—five minutes!—we can play hangman the rest of the period.

Incredibly, this works. The five kids stare down at their blank sheets of paper and begin to write.

In a show of solidarity, I pull out a blank piece of paper, too. "My Perfect Saturday," I write at the top. I stare at the sheet of paper in front of me, at its eternal blank whiteness, its sea of possibilities. And nothing comes. For the life of me, I can't come up with a single sentence to describe my perfect Saturday, mainly because I have no idea what my perfect Saturday would look like. A day with Ray? A day with Chad? A day alone? I'm worse off than I thought I was. I don't know at all what I want.

Five minutes later, five papers are flung onto my desk and hangman begins. Jonathan goes first. In two guesses we've unmasked his letters: SCHOOL SUCKS.

Tom, it turns out, had a marvelous visit with his family back in Pittsburgh over Thanksgiving break and, it turns out, even had time, it turns out, to look up an old girlfriend who, it turns out, is recently divorced and feeling a bit shaky lately and, it turns out, is thrilled to have heard from good old Tom from the old days, the same Tom she unceremoniously dumped in order to marry the asshole who, it turns out, left her for a younger woman. And believe it or not, this old girlfriend, who, it turns out, just now had the epiphany of a lifetime, which is that Tom is the man she should have married instead of the asshole— well, believe it or not, this very same old girlfriend is coming to visit, it turns out, very soon. As in very, very soon. As in next week soon.

And Tom will bring her to work so that everyone can meet her.

Elsa spent the weekend shopping.

The next week, Tom shows up in the teacher's lounge all pasty-faced and loose-bodied, the way I have always imagined he would look in the morning after a full night of nonstop sexual adventuring. He goes to pour himself a cup of burnt coffee from the ancient pocked pot that has sat in the teacher's lounge for all my twelve years at Thomas Alva Edison Intermediate School without, as far as I know, ever being cleaned, and spills most of what's left in the pot onto the counter. I can't stand to look at him.

Elsa: So things are going good, huh?

His tired lips have barely enough energy left to give a tiny perk at the corners. His eyes are so hooded they might as well be shut. He's blindly, blatantly in love with his old girlfriend, and even though I am blindly and blatantly in love with my old boyfriend, somehow our similar circumstances feel like wholly different entities, as if my obsession is sensible and understandable while his is merely an early-midlife-crisis event and not to be taken seriously. I feel like slapping some sense into him. Instead, I pretend that I've got something more pressing awaiting me in the resource room than my morning paper and half a cup of cold coffee, and take off down the hall.

It doesn't take much to talk Gwen into going to the movies to sneak a peek at Tom and his old girlfriend, who is rapidly, it seems, becoming his current girlfriend, if his disheveled, dumbly happy-feet appearance at work is any indication.

We arrive at the theater early and sit in the very center seats of the center row, something I never get to do on those rare occasions when Jim and I actually agree on a movie to see together, since Jim must always always always sit near the front and on the side and in the aisle seat of his side row, no matter what. It's one of his things— one of those many pesky compromises that married couples are supposed to find worth compromising on for the sake of the marriage, but also one of those compromises that I find incredibly annoying if not downright pathologically sick on my husband's part. Would it kill him to just once sit in the middle of the theater the way normal people do? Is that such a terrible, horrible thing to consider doing? Must he be *that* stuck in his routine that I must suffer through every movie with my neck craned to the side so that my entire concentration eventually shifts from any thoughts of the movie to only thoughts about how fucking stiff my neck feels? Can I never just face forward like the rest of the civilized world?

We spread our things out around the adjoining seats and throw our coats over the seats directly in front of us and break into our packs of Red Vines. I've never even heard of this movie. Something obscure. French, I think. Or Italian.

You sure he's coming to this one? Gwen whispers.

That's what he said.

Tell me what I'm looking for.

Bald, I say.

Gwen turns her head slowly and takes a peek behind us.

Lots of bald guys, she says.

I turn to look and find jutting from the sea of seats a smattering of men in various stages of hair loss. Have there always been so many bald men around? I have that feeling you get when you learn a new word and it starts popping up everywhere.

Wrong bald guys, I say.

A minute later, Tom and his old girlfriend fly past us down the aisle and head toward the front. Without any conferencing about the selection, they slide into seats in the absolute center of the row, then slump down low into them. Tom is wearing a sweatshirt with a hood and looks about fifteen years old except for the no-hair part. The old girlfriend is way too cute, all small and sneakered and teensy glasses and long hair in one messy braid. And young! She's got a good ten years of braid wearing left before someone kindly informs her that it's about time she cut her hair. I'm certain she smells of patchouli.

The old girlfriend turns to say something to Tom with her face no more than two millimeters away from his. I have no choice but to hope the movie is filled with gratuitous violence.

One morning in December, I know I'm pregnant. I wake up and just know. I have that feeling in my gut that comes with the sinking realization that things will never be the same. Not one ounce of me feels happiness. I'm nothing but a lump of dread. It seems utterly impossible and utterly possible in the same instant. The fact of it is obvious and crystal-clear to the same extent that the biological origins are a total blur. I play everything over and over inside my head. I make mental calculations and more mental calculations, and then I make the same mental calculations all over again. I get out a pen and a pad of paper and a calculator and peck away at numbers and more numbers and more numbers. And each time I come up with the same thing.

I don't know who the father is. It would be funny if only it were funny. But it's not.

When I told Jim I was pregnant the first time—with Chad, that is—he surprised me by being happy about it. We'd never discussed having children. We'd never even discussed getting married. We were boyfriend and girlfriend, with room to spare for the occasional fling with someone else. Semi-attached. An almost couple. Together enough to make weekend plans in advance, but not together enough to plan a life together.

Nevertheless, Jim thought it was all great. He doesn't believe in accidents. He decided the baby was meant to be. We didn't discuss abortion even once.

You'll be a great mother, he told me.

Which is really about the nicest thing he ever said to me, even if it wasn't quite on the money.

Something tells me that with this current pregnancy, I'm not going to get a similar happy reaction. So I decide to hold on to the news for a while longer. With how little attention he's paid to me since our big weekend in Cannon Beach, maybe he won't even notice.

As natural and necessary for propagation as pregnancy is, it still seems like the weirdest thing in the world. How is it possible for the human body to do something so miraculous without the slightest bit of conscious knowledge about how, exactly, to do it? How can something so profound be so humdrum, so everyday, so nothing-really-to-it?

These are the kinds of thoughts that invade my brain and turn me into Cosmic Pregnant Lady. Being fruitful and multiplying does that to me. But it's true, isn't it? That one long line of humanity stretches back through the eons, all the way back to the first human couple doing their primal, doggy-style thing in the primordial dust, starting the whole ball of DNA rolling down to me? And here I go, laying the entire heavy load on another human being without asking permission first. It's way too easy to go from fucking to fucking someone up.

Among the things the books don't tell you: When you finally release the huge, unsightly volleyball that is your baby from between your huge, unsightly thighs, it will look as though there is something terribly wrong with it even if there isn't. That's what happened with Chad. I can't really speak for all the other mothers out there, who give birth to perfect angel-faced babies, and accept their precious lump of pinkness into their open arms with a wide, loving smile, sure of themselves and their ability to care for the little screaming thing. I suppose scenarios like that happen all the time.

Chad looked funny. Chad definitely looked major-league weird, his lips about five times too big for his face, so that they formed a wrinkled line like the mouth of an oyster shell. And his balls were as red as a fire truck. Is that normal? That's what I screamed out a few hundred times as they wiped him, weighed him, and did whatever it is they do to newborn babies the moment they are born, to determine whether or not the news is good. No one answered. This should be illegal. Nurses and doctors and stand-around orderlies should be required to answer a hysterical new mother when she asks: Is he normal? Day one of medical school should start with this very subject. Rule number one: Calm the new mother when she is hysterically screaming, Is he normal? Is he? *Well, is he?*

Rule number two: New fathers are required to stay with new mothers until released from the task of staying. New fathers should, by no means, immediately go to the one-hour photo shop and immediately get the photographs developed of the Chad-thing being birthed and immediately show them to a million people, some of whom the new mother must look in the face in the very near future, without first inquiring of the new mother whether or not she minds if millions of people view her wide-open vagina and huge, flabby white thighs and incredibly swollen ankles in stark, no-holds-barred photographic glory.

Under no circumstances should the new father show up at the hospital looking tired and stressed and wanting comfort from the new mother. Under no circumstances should the new father expect to still be able to attend a Sonics basketball game with his buddies the very next evening because, as he tells the new mother, he might not be able to get out with his buddies for a while. Under no circumstances should the new father complain, albeit with a smirking half-smile on his face, about the fact that the new mother had the audacity to actually throw up on him during the birth process, as if she had any choice in the matter. Under no circumstances should the new father remark to the new mother in a throwaway manner, as if it didn't mean a thing, that it's really quite fascinating how a woman can give birth to an eight-pound, twelve-ounce baby and still look like she's pregnant! How hilarious!

* * *

I'm staring at the Mack truck of a vitamin on my kitchen counter and wondering how in God's name a pregnant woman could possibly be expected to swallow such an enormous, foul-smelling object, when the phone rings. It's my mother calling to say she feels pain behind her ears and also in the back of her gums and she thinks the nodules in her neck are swelling up because of that and not because she has cancer, right? And do I ever get that same thing, the lymph nodes in my neck swelling up like little peas at first and then more like round gumballs? I tell her, Ma, it's nothing, it will go away in a few days, stop worrying about it, it's your body's natural defenses doing their natural defensive job against some weak invader, all the while knowing that the very minute I hang up, my own neck will have a host of little swollen peas settling in for a long-term stay, necessitating a doctor's appointment, the morning of which the peas will miraculously disappear, although I will still be charged for the appointment, seeing as how I didn't give twenty-four hours' notice for the cancellation.

You're not dying, I tell my mother, already hearing the eulogies at my own funeral. Already wondering if Ray will show up to weep over my coffin.

Chad wants to borrow money. For Christmas presents, he says. What a brilliant kid I have raised. I fork over a hundred dollars, knowing I'll never see more than a bag of Reese's peanut butter cups under the tree Christmas morning.

Later, Gwen calls to say her husband has walked out on her without warning.

Why? I ask.

Gwen is panting on the other end of the line. I picture her wearing that absurd headset she bought so she could chat away while folding her laundry or doing dishes, all the while looking either like Madonna in concert or else a travel agent, depending on what she's wearing.

He didn't say anything, she finally spits out. He just left.

He must have said something.

No.

A person doesn't just walk out without saying anything.

Silence. More panting. Small squeaking sounds, like a mouse trapped in a cupboard.

Gwen?

He met someone, she says.

And so the *Wizard of Oz* Theory of Life comes to a tearful and bitter end. Gwen's husband, as it turns out, didn't look in his own backyard, didn't learn that there's no place like home, didn't use his midlife crisis to find out everything he thought he wanted was right where he'd left it, back in Kansas. No, Gwen's husband got a brain and a heart and the courage to tell Gwen he'd fallen for his receptionist, yes, the one with the tattoo of a butterfly on her neck, even though he'd always said he hated tattoos, especially on women, but you know, he sees things differently now because Bethany has opened his eyes to a whole new world, a world miles and miles away from Kansas and Gwen and the two boys, who, he hopes, will someday forgive him.

Remember that he smelled bad, I tell Gwen.

This, however, is not the thing she wants to hear, meaning my streak of ill-timed social comments is still intact. In the world of the faux pas, I bat a perfect one thousand.

He didn't, she says. I only said he did.

9

All December it rains. And pours. And then rains some more. And then it seems to stop, but it's only a false hope because it starts to pour again, and then sprinkle, and then drop sideways.

Ray says, It's not raining here. The sun is out. It's another beautiful California day.

He doesn't really say it. I only imagine him saying it during one of the many imaginary phone calls that always ends with Ray's telling me that now, with Jim dead in that horrible car crash neither of us had any control over, now that I am alone in the world and unattached and so, amazingly, is he, now is the time for the two of us to begin our life together, don't I agree? After which I feel terrible for killing off Jim in an imaginary car wreck.

I know a woman whose husband died and left her alone to raise their three-year-old son in their tastefully furnished home, along with two cars, a condo at Sun Valley, and an insurance policy to keep her in fat city for the rest of her life. Isn't that really every woman's fantasy? That her husband would die and leave her everything and she wouldn't have to go through a messy divorce and also wouldn't have to live with him forever and put up with doing his laundry and dealing with his parents, and cooking things with no dairy products for every meal because he's goddamn lactose-intolerant? He dies, and everyone feels bad, and she comes out still young and beautiful and, even more than that, tragic. She is a young, beautiful thing, touched by tragedy, and able to do things like sleep with her now married ex-boyfriend from high school after finding him standing behind her in line for the chair lift at Sun Valley, and she doesn't even have to feel bad about doing it! He's the one who's still married! Let him feel like shit the next day! She doesn't have to! Her husband's kicked the bucket!

She may not admit it, but deep down in every woman's heart, such a fantasy exists.

* * *

At the newspaper holiday party, Jim is a wreck. He cuts his prime rib into bits and pieces, and shoves them around his plate until the tiny pink slabs land hurricane-fashion everywhere, dotting his peas and carrots, decorating his potatoes, hiding under a couple of white dinner rolls slathered in butter. It's performance art, a piece of anguish at the sight of Patricia laughing merrily three tables away, her black dress purposefully revealing a pair of unblemished, haughty breasts, and short enough at the thigh to earn a trip to the principal's office. The server asks Jim if he's finished at least four times before Jim finally relinquishes his plate.

And then Patricia is dancing with red-faced, alcohol-drenched Brad—more than that, is slithering across the dance floor, her mouth hanging open in a smile far too big for this universe. Is that really attractive? Is the fact that she's almost, but not quite, fully dressed really acceptable? Shouldn't someone, somewhere, do her the favor of slapping her hard across the cheek to wake her from her Victoria's Secret Catalogue dreamworld?

Next thing you know, my husband has cut in on Brad's action to dance maniacally in Patricia's personal space, an annoying mosquito hoping to latch on to her skin. Except that Patricia doesn't look in the least bit annoyed. On the contrary, she looks ready to lick my husband's face in rhythm to his worshipful jig to her melon-sized jugs. Then they disappear into the crowd and I lose track of the both of them.

Brad collapses in the chair next to me, the sweat lifting from his body like puffs of steam.

Your husband! he shouts at me.

What? I shout back.

Your husband! Brad yells in my ear. What an asshole!

I find Jim a good twenty minutes later, sharing a smoke with Patricia on the deck, where the pariah smokers have landed for the evening to do their pariah smoking. My husband does not smoke. He looks up at me sheepishly, a bluish cloud encircling him like a lifesaving device, a cigarette held uncomfortably between his fingers.

Ready to go? he asks, as though he'd only been waiting for me to finish up some last-minute business before we can head home.

I decide to go through all of Jim's drawers. I decide not to. Repeat.

Ray may have entered my life with a bang, but Jim came out of left field, a blur in my peripheral vision, a blip on my radar, a subliminal message in the otherwise banal film strip of my life. Just another passably good-looking guy in a pair of black jeans and a white T-shirt, emptying his garbage in the basement of the building where we both lived, grabbing his mail from his box in the lobby, buying grapefruits at Safeway at eleven p.m. Then, one gloomy Saturday in late winter, while poking at a plate of eggs at the Continental restaurant at two in the afternoon, drinking from my fiftieth cup of coffee of the day, smoking my thousandth cigarette, and trying to remember the guy I was trying to forget, the guy I'd slept with the night before—trying to remember how it happened that I'd asked him back to my apartment, when I had promised myself never, ever again to ask a half-stranger who faintly resembled Ray to come back to my apartment to spend half the night poorly imitating the man I was, in fact, still in love with—out of nowhere a voice arose, asking to borrow my ketchup. I glanced up. It was the guy from my building. We'd never spoken before.

Sure, I said.

I didn't know that our separate lives had in that moment intersected to form an initial point of reference on the graph of our relationship. All I knew was that as he leaned across my table to fetch the bottle of ketchup from between the Tabasco and the salt and pepper shakers, he suddenly clicked into focus.

* * *

I didn't see him again until Deborah on the fourth floor had a dinner party and invited the both of us. He wasn't my type, which is another way of saying he clearly wasn't Ray, but he had a certain skinny-guy charm to him. He'd baked a loaf of zucchini bread, which weighed about ten pounds and looked like a football wrapped in foil, which upped his charm quotient even further. He wore a wrinkled white button-down shirt and managed to look right in it. He was a few years older, but not too old. Mostly, he was funny. Really goddamn funny. I hadn't realized that I'd been looking for a funny guy before. I hadn't noticed how long it had been since I'd had a good laugh.

I found myself thinking about him the next day, remembering the way his small white teeth sloped inward, and the way he kept his hair cropped short so that his perfect ears were exposed to the world. He had a nice face. Even unshaven, he looked clean.

A few nights later, he took me out for Chinese food. I'm the worst person in the world to go out for Chinese food with, in that I eat only the chicken dishes, and only mild chicken dishes at that, but Jim didn't seem to mind. Nor did he mind that I smoked about twenty cigarettes before our food came. He even smoked one himself. He didn't mind when I said that I loved watching television and that I didn't like to go hiking and that I liked nothing more than a good glazed doughnut for breakfast. He didn't care that I was too skinny and that my boobs were too small and my nose was too big and my laugh was too loud. In fact, he liked all of those things. Or he said he did.

He took me back to his apartment, and I was relieved to find he was all right to sleep with. Soon enough, he was my boyfriend. And for a while, I forgot about Ray. Or didn't forget, actually, but folded him up and set him aside, while I discovered someone new.

Jim. Jim. Jim. I tried to get used to it. I didn't like it especially. It wasn't a name I would have chosen for a boyfriend. I called him James for a while, but it always sounded like I was joking, which, in fact, I was. I tried Jamie, and Jamester, and Jim-Bob, and Jim-bub and Jimmy Boy. Nothing took. I tried a different tack. I called him something else altogether. I called him Jorge. After a while, it morphed into Georgie, and then just plain George. From there, it became Jimmy-George, which soon shortened to Jimmy, which, after a while, further reduced itself to Jim. And there I was, back where I'd started. Except I liked the name better.

* * *

We dinked around together for a few months. He was a pretty good boyfriend. But the fact of the matter is that if I hadn't gotten pregnant with Chad, the two of us would have never gotten married. We both know it, even though we don't say it out loud. If I hadn't gotten pregnant, we would have lasted another three months, four months, tops. We were on the downhill slide at that point. We were pretty close to the bottom of things. The novelty had worn off. Ray was lurking about, waiting to surface. I'd started to do the thing I always did, which was to compare the way Jim did things with the way Ray did things. Dangerous territory.

And then I was pregnant.

Let's get married, Jim said. Let's buy a house.

And honest to God, I thought, Here's my one chance for a normal life, a Rayless life, a husband-and-two-car-garage-and-swingset-in-the-backyard life. Honest to God, I thought, It's marry Jim or lose any hope of being married, forever. So, I figured, what the hell.

Not the best goddamn reason to get married.

And Chad turned out to be my favorite person in the universe. Sure, I'd heard all about maternal bonding and the power of motherly love and that you never, ever in all your life will possibly ever love another person as much as you will love your own child, but I didn't get it until Chad appeared. And he didn't even have to do anything. He could just be sleeping and I'd be mad for him. He could be picking his nose or banging a block on the coffee table or dropping Cheerios on the floor. Have you ever watched your own child drop Cheerios on the floor? There is not a more beautiful, amazing show in the universe than your sweet, perfect child plucking a single Cheerio from his high-chair tray, moving his hand through space as he clutches that single piece of cereal between his tiny pinched fingers, and then opening those fingers with total sincere delight, allowing that single Cheerio to nose-dive to the floor, laughing at the sight, at the sound, at the look on his mother's face at his accomplishing such a feat of dexterity, and then, almost immediately, pressing his lips together, looking down at his tray, picking out his next Cheerio victim for imminent destruction. Spend five minutes watching your own child do this and you will be done for. Gone. Taken. Smitten. Smote. Your heart tied up forever. The old Cheerio trick. They all know it.

For a while, it seemed to work. We bought a house on the edge of the city. Jim worked downtown at the newspaper and I stayed home, trying my best to figure out how in the world to be a mother. It's not like I had anything decent to go on. It's not like I was going to ask my own mother for advice on mothering. I ended up buying a library of parenting books and reading every fucking one of them. For anyone who is thinking of doing the same, allow me to summarize: Sleeping with your baby is good. Sleeping with your baby is bad. Schedules, yes. Schedules, no. Lay them on their stomachs. Lay them on their backs. Bottle. Breast. Wean. Don't wean. Toilet train. Don't toilet train. Pick them up when they cry. Never pick up a crying baby. Public school. Home school. Montessori. Competitive sports are good. Competitive sports are bad. Fluoride. No fluoride. Vaccines. No vaccines.

You're welcome.

After the fog of the first couple of years of Chad's life, things started to clear up. I woke one morning miserably aware that I was married to the wrong man, raising a child with no idea what I was doing, and unhappily padding around my house in pajamas all day, waiting for God knows what to happen. It occurred to me that I was seriously depressed. I didn't know what in the world I should do.

The little guy made me crazy with worry. I watched

him all day like a hawk. I watched him chew every nugget of food, made certain he swallowed without choking. I followed him from room to room. Watched on television whatever he was watching. Checked on him over and over while he slept. Held my breath as he played in the park, trying to keep track of all things at once—the play structure he might fall from, the other kids who might bully him, the child-snatcher who might be lurking in the bushes. One day, not two feet away from me, he fell, for no reason. He simply fell, flat on his face, in the middle of the kitchen floor, and broke one of his front teeth. That was it. It was with massive relief that I enrolled him in an all-day preschool. I couldn't take it anymore.

I went to work in the resource room watching other people's children. Other people's children were not a problem for me.

10

At work, I pick Tom's name out of the hat for Secret Santas. When I read his name on the slip of paper, it hits me that my crush is over. His name means nothing to me now. Only Tom, as in good old bald Tom. It's something of a disappointment to find that the thrill is gone. Instead of a rush in my stomach at the thought of buying a secret gift for my secret beloved, there is only the relief at having never let on in any obvious way to my now fleeting devotion. After much deliberation, which means the five minutes it takes me to come across it in Rite Aid, I buy him a baseball cap inscribed with the words "Wish You Were Hair."

The funny part about having a crush on someone and

then losing your crush on that person is that the moment you start to wonder what ever came over you to find a poorly dressed, narrow-shouldered, weak-willed, nearly bald guy attractive in the first place will turn out to be the exact moment when the poorly dressed, narrow-shouldered, weak-willed, nearly bald guy suddenly notices your existence.

Not that I think Tom has a thing for me. But you'd call this attention, right? The other day, in the teacher's lounge, as I'm picking between my front teeth with the edge of a Snickers wrapper, Tom starts smiling at me from across the table.

What? I ask him.

You know, you have nice teeth, he says.

And I am just pathetic enough to let that half-pint-sized compliment replay itself over and over inside my head for the rest of the day.

Christmas is at Stacy's. I spend much of the morning telling myself that the sick feeling in my stomach is just a reaction to my mother's perfume, nothing more. I refuse to allow morning sickness this time around. That's all there is to it.

Chad startles me by giving me a very nice wool sweater, a shape I never wear, but which I throw on immediately over my shirt out of total delight. Jim gives me pajamas and candlesticks and a gift certificate for a massage. I give him books on gardening, and gardening gloves and gardening tools. Stacy gives me a book for parents of adolescents that I will never read, mostly because Stacy gives it to me and I refuse to read anything that Stacy gives me. My mother gives me a pair of earrings that are surprisingly not ugly.

It's overall a nice-enough scene, and I waste only about half of it wondering who it is Ray is spending the day with in California.

The next morning there is a huge mother of a fly crawling across my bedroom window, looking for an escape. Back and forth it crawls, over and over.

You idiot, I say to the fly.

In the afternoon, it expires on the windowsill, six legs pointing toward the sky.

Well, well, well, I say to the fly corpse. Should have flown when you had the chance.

I spend that afternoon at Gwen's, watching the dustballs in the corners of her living room grow to *Guinness Book of*

World Records size. Gwen has stopped cleaning. She's basically stopped cooking, too, except for anything that can be microwaved. She's become adept at picking clothes up off the floor, brushing them off with a smack of her hand, and calling them clean. Her kids don't know what to make of her, but they aren't asking any questions. They are smart enough to move around the personal-space boundaries she has set since her husband decamped, namely, anywhere within fifty feet of their mother.

Gwen, who has always smoked but who has always pretended to have no idea how that pack of Marlboro Lights made its way into her purse, now smokes openly and with great panache, holding her cigarettes delicately between her long, spooky fingers, drawing in smoke in great, dramatic inhalations and then blowing it out again toward the ceiling. She jabs at the air with her lit cigarettes, swearing at her husband. Gwen was born to smoke.

We watch the phone men fixing the phone lines on the street and spend a couple of hours deciding which one of us gets which man. We both like best the one we've named Phil, but I relent and let Gwen have him.

Gwen tells me a good story. It's about carpeting, although of course it has nothing at all to do with carpeting and everything to do with what an asshole Bill always was but she was just too blind to see it. What happened was that Gwen and her husband had had a few million conversations about carpeting the dining room floor, conversations that spread out over the course of probably a year and that always culminated in the same decision: No carpeting. Gwen emphasizes this strongly to me, how completely the two of them had worked over this household drama of carpet-versus-no-carpet and how completely the two of them had firmly decided against it. And then Gwen came back from a week away, visiting her mother in Cleveland—a week in which she called home every morning and every night, conversations that bore no clue as to what was happening to her dining room floor in her absence, simply complacent everyday conversations, sprinkled with the usual "I love you" and "Miss you" and that sort of thing—Gwen came back from this innocent week away in Cleveland to find that her husband had carpeted the dining room floor. Wall-to-wall. Navy blue. Carpet.

I should have known right then, Gwen says.

Chad and Tricia have broken up. I know this not because my son comes and offers this piece of information, but because he is suddenly home all the time, eating all the good stuff in the cupboards and ignoring all the more healthy, organic items that I purchase just to know that I have purchased them but that I never have any real intentions of eating. And he is suddenly up in his bedroom for hours on end, playing obscenely loud bass-driven CDs and lighting incense to cover the smell of his pot, an old trick that has never fooled anyone since first attempted at the dawn of the millennium. But I appreciate the effort.

Answering machine message number one:

It's me. Your mother. I wish you were there, but you're not. Well. Okay. You're not there. Okay. I'll call again later when you're home. Well, I hope you'll be home. Or that Chad will be home. Gosh, he looked nice on Christmas, didn't he? Nice boy. I've always said he's a nice boy. But what I wanted to ask you, but you're not there so I can't, what I wanted to know is if you ever get this sort of sore throat that isn't all that sore but is more like very, very dry, and you have to cough when you don't need to cough, but you cough anyway? Do you get that? [Cough] Because I don't know if I should see a doctor or not. Do you think it could be strep? Because that's what I'm most afraid of. That it could be strep and then if I don't do anything about it, you know how strep can go to your heart, right? I forget what it's called, but I know that untreated strep can do something bad to your
[Beep]
Answering machine message number two:

I don't know, I guess I got cut off. [Cough] Anyway, I suppose I was done anyway. So call me, will you? Have you worn the earrings yet?

Ray finally calls, two weeks after Christmas. He's drunk. He likes to call me when he's been drinking. Likes to inform me that he loves me.

God, he says. God, I love you.

I want to hang up on him for not calling sooner, but since he had no idea he was supposed to call me sooner I don't. I want to tell him that I'm pregnant, but I don't do that, either. Drunk as he is, he might not remember any of this in the morning. So, I only listen while he launches into his usual drunken diatribe, sucking in as many calories from it as possible. I'm beneath pathetic.

I'm such an idiot, he tells me.

But what he also wants to tell me, he just remembered, is that he's coming to town in a couple of weeks and could I maybe work it out so that we might be able to get together for coffee or something?

Of course, I can't help wondering at that or-something part.

* * *

You learn something new every day. Here's what I learn from the girl with platinum hair who makes me a double tall nonfat decaf mocha, no foam, at the coffee shop where I'm supposed to meet Ray. First of all, that almond biscotti are a better food choice in terms of calories and health than a bagel. She says she read it in a magazine this very morning. Almond biscotti. Who knew?

And then, after a few conversational back-and-forths about our bodies and how much we dislike them, followed by a few more back-and-forths about how the other one of us looks great, she tells me that she's a bit ticked off this afternoon because her husband informed her just last night that he's been keeping track of every time they've had sex in the last three months. Every time. And not just a mental calculation on his part. No, he's kept a little notebook, and every time they had intercourse he made a little check mark and every time they had oral sex he made a little star, and as it turns out, there are absolutely no stars in the entire notebook, and only twelve little check marks, all on the same page. Twelve.

I'm stumped as to how to respond. But more than that, I'm doing some very swift mental calculations of my own, attempting to come up with a more or less accurate number of how many little check marks Jim might have been able to put down in a little notebook over the last three months if he, in fact, felt like keeping track of such things. And I'm unable to get past four little check marks, and truth be known, a couple of those would have to be very small and awfully quick.

And while I toy with the thought of passing along this piece of information to the girl behind the counter as payback for the almond biscotti tip, Ray suddenly materializes behind me, slipping his hands around my waist and kissing my neck. So all I can do is give the girl what I hope comes off as a comforting smile and wait for her to take Ray's coffee order.

He's less tan than he was at the wedding. He's got a new haircut, shorter, more stylish. He's wearing a fleece jacket, a pair of old jeans. On his feet, running sneakers. No socks. He looks fit. He looks like he's about to set off on an outdoors adventure. He's brought me a present: a fleece pullover in turquoise with lavender piping. This is what he does these days, sells fleece. He's made a small fortune as owner of a company that makes high-end fleece products for people who want to look as though they'd just come back from a sail around the globe or a trek in the Himalayas. For people who want to look like Ray.

Put it on, he instructs me.

I toss on the pullover and twirl in front of him. I still don't look pregnant. It's early yet.

You look great, he says. You really do.

We finish our coffees and drive in Ray's truck to my house. He wants to see where I live before we head over to Melissa and Greg's for what he's told me is a get-together with old friends. We take the scenic route, which means the route where we are least likely to pass anyone I might know, which means a very convoluted ride of twists and turns on streets I am barely familiar with, until at last we pull into the driveway of my house and Ray cuts the engine. He peers up at our charming Tudor-style home. He doesn't say anything. I look at what he is looking at and find that my house suddenly seems very conservative. Jim's lawn is hideously manicured. The shrubs have been sheared into lonely humps. I can't believe I live here, of all places. Suburbia.

So this is it, Ray says finally.

I shake my head. Yeah, I say.

We go inside. I'm all at once in a bit of a sweat. I'm feeling guilty about bringing him into my house. Listen, I know how dumb that sounds. Here I've let Ray into my vagina without so much as a backward glance, and yet I'm in a sweat over letting him into my living room. It doesn't help that now it seems way too late to pop the baby news. Could I get you a glass of lemonade? Oh, and did I mention that I'm pregnant? And that you are quite possibly the father?

You okay? Ray asks me.

I'm fine, I say, a little too quickly.

It occurs to me that the chances that Gwen is watching us from the vantage point of her living room window are probably pretty close to one hundred percent. Bringing Ray to the old homestead was a terrible idea, all the way around. I make one great sweeping motion with my arm, inviting him to take in the sights of my living room.

Okay, I say. Let's go.

When we arrive at Melissa and Greg's for the so-called get-together with old friends, no one is there except Melissa and Greg. There is no get-together with old friends. It's only me and Ray and Melissa and Greg—two couples sitting around the dinner table just like old times, before all the shit that became my life began.

Thought you said it was a party, I say when Greg and Melissa have departed to the kitchen to make dinner.

Ray takes one hand and swipes at the hair next to my ear, and my insides shiver, a fact I find slightly embarrassing, knowing as I do that Ray's patented hair swipe has been bought and sold to dozens of women over the years. Still, it works.

I never said a big party, Ray says.

Melissa and Greg are sickeningly happy together. They slap at each other with kitchen towels. They laugh at each other's jokes. They do not make pointed comments whose purpose is to reveal their dissatisfaction with each other. Over the fireplace, a picture shows the two of them on their wedding day, laughing in raucous fashion as they feed each other a bite of wedding cake. It's the kind of picture that makes other couples painfully aware of their own despair.

They have made sushi themselves. And cream puffs. They serve a brand of beer that they discovered while biking in Germany last summer. No one seems to notice when I decline on the beer.

Melissa and Greg's guest room in the basement is fit only for the hardy, musty and freezing as it is. There's not much to cheer the place up. An old futon covered in layers of sleeping bags and comforters; a couple of undersized pillows drowning in their cases. And Ray's stuff—he's staying with them while he's here—forming a familiar wrinkled pile in one corner, a jumble of jeans and T-shirts and thick wool sweaters that I recognize as his mother's handiwork. I pick up a forest-green one and shake it out.

You ought to give her some grandchildren to knit for, I say.

Ray ignores the comment.

Got something to show you, he says.

He reaches into the back pocket of his jeans, pulls out

his wallet, and flips it open to a pair of pictures he's cropped to fit into the windows.

Look, he says.

The first one's of me, an earlier version of me, the old Julia, the skinny, long-haired, smiling Julia of long ago, wearing a turquoise shirt and faded jeans, looking at the camera, or more accurately, looking at Ray behind the camera with a look that says, As soon as you put that camera down I'm going to fuck you big-time. And next to the picture of the old Julia is a picture of the old Ray and Julia, my forehead against his shoulder, my hand set on his bare, tanned chest, Ray talking to someone, his hand in the air, his hair golden and tousled. I've got the same picture tucked away in the back of my file cabinet at home.

Nice pictures, I say. I don't say: Why in the world would you still, after all these years, be carrying around those pictures of me and you in your wallet? I don't say: This is insane, that you would still, after all these years, be carrying around those pictures of me and you in your wallet. I don't say: For Christ's sake, what kind of past are you living in, keeping pictures of the two of us in your wallet as if we were still some sort of a couple? I'm married, you idiot. I have a fifteen-year-old kid and a mortgage. I don't say: I'm carrying a child and it very well could be yours. I don't say anything at all. I just let Ray pull me down onto the futon and remove my clothes. When you're already pregnant, it's the simplest thing in the world to do.

After weeks of weighing tactics and waiting for the right moment, I finally go and blow it entirely by announcing my knocked-up state to my husband with two minutes to go, no time-outs left, Sonics up by one.

Jim, I say. I'm going to have a baby.

Jim flings out an arm into the blank air in front of him, the universal sign for "Shut the fuck up, can't you see this is a very important game?"

Jim, did you hear me?

Furious second arm-fling. Followed by sharp intake of breath. Followed by momentary catatonia. Followed by utter speechlessness. Followed by, Are you sure? Followed by face in hands. Followed by severe head-shaking, with face still held in hands. Followed by something else that I didn't witness, because I'd already left the room.

A few minutes later, he finds me up in our bedroom. He has more or less regained his composure, although his hair is sticking straight up on the top of his head from his running his palms through it a few hundred times. He looks like the maniacal serial killer in a teenage horror flick, but without the carving knife.

Who won? I ask.

Stop it, he says.

He stands just inside the doorway, hands on his hips.

Well? he says.

Well what?

What are we going to do?

I can't tell if he's angry or just in shock. He's certainly not happy. I can tell that much.

I'm going to have it, I tell him.

Are you?

Yes.

That's it? You tell me you're going to have it and that's it?

I guess so.

Well, that's just great, he says. That's just fucking fantastic.

He walks out of the room, leaving me alone with my

inhabited belly. Lately I've found myself enamored of the little alien doing flip-flops beneath my navel. I've grown fond of the little pink unit.

You're a keeper, I tell it.

Since when are there so many volumes of baby-name books in the parenting aisle of Barnes & Noble?

I draw one of the books from a shelf and look up *Chad.* "Origin cloudy," it says, as though I couldn't have told them that myself. "Fierce."

"Will find you inadequate," I want to scratch in the margin. "Will spend thousands of dollars in therapy in the future, discussing your shortcomings."

Names I won't be considering:

Atlas, Coburn, Dexter, Gifford, Harlow, Jenkins, Linford, Primo, Thaddeus.

Bettina, Chesney, Elba, Gunhilda, Jovita, Lorelle, Myrtle, Prunella, Therma.

Jim says nothing more until the following afternoon. Then he calls me at home, where I am trying unsuccessfully to nap.

Look, he says. I don't think this is a unilateral thing. I

don't think you just get to tell me that we're having another kid without my having some input into the decision. I just don't think that's fair.

I'm sorry, I say. I really am.

He sighs loudly and then the two of us sit there for a while, not talking.

Finally Jim says, I'm sorry too, and hangs up the phone.

I have a quiet moment. I lie on my bed with my hands over my belly. I close my eyes and breathe deeply. I tell the alien: I don't care where you came from. You are mine. You are loved. You are perfect. Even if you turn out to have one of those horrible defects the genetic counselor will surely warn us about, you are still perfect. I, Cosmic Pregnant Lady, deem it so.

What is so goddamn shocking, I'd like to know.

Elsa: A baby? You're kidding.

Chad: Aren't you kind of old for this?

My mother: Don't play with me.

Jim's father: Well, well, well.

Jim's mother: Wha?

Stacy: No!

Tom: Is this a good thing?

Tina: This wasn't planned, was it?

Diane: I don't know what to say. I mean, congratulations, right?

Ray: [Silence, seeing as how I haven't told him yet]

It appears that I've got three options: Tell Ray that I'm pregnant and that Jim is the father. Tell Ray that I'm pregnant and that it's possible he's the father. Don't tell Ray anything.

Being the chickenshit we all know and love, for the time being I go with option number three.

There are no other roads of thought. No alternative pathways. Wars, bombings, terrorist threats—what are these in comparison with the tiny, alien pink thing of half-uncertain origin swimming inside me, oblivious of the insanity of the outside world, its only task to divide and multiply, to feed off the keeling mother ship?

At work, Elsa tells me she's stopped shaving her pubic hair. After years of the full-Brazilian, she can't get over it—the look of her vulva with a covering of soft fur.

It's like an animal, she says. Like having a wee creature living down there.

I don't know what I would do without Elsa around to say and think things that even I wouldn't say or think. I know that using Elsa as a meter to my sanity is cheating a little, since she's so offbeat she probably wouldn't register on the scale. But she's available, and she's awfully consistent in her output, so I'll keep using her.

Claude is getting used to it, she tells me.

I'm suddenly paranoid about the resource room. Everything in it looks suspiciously germ-laden. Especially the kids. I decide to do a unit on cleanliness and hygiene. This unit will have to be covert, of course, since units on cleanliness and hygiene are not in my job description. I say things like: Keep your hands away from your face. Or: Did you wash your hands? Or: Are you sure you washed your hands? Or: Maybe you'd like to wash your hands before touching my desk.

I carry a box of tissues around with me, offering them at will.

I'm maybe three months pregnant when it occurs to Elsa that Ray may, in fact, be the father. She is unexpectedly horrified.

You have to find out, she says. You can't just raise a child without knowing who the dad is. What if there's some genetic thing you have to know about? What if Ray gets Huntington's disease or something? What if Jim needs a new kidney and the mystery child offers to donate one? What if it's a boy who looks exactly like Ray? Do you really think no one will notice he's got shoulders the size of a ship? A head of blond hair?

Stress is not good for pregnant mothers, I tell her.

But she's right. It's time to tell Ray. And not only to be prepared in the event of some awful medical emergency, either. I want his honest response. It seems to me that his response will make a difference, will help settle things in my brain. Not that I have any idea what kind of response I want him to have. Anger? No, I don't want him to be angry. Happiness? Might my pregnancy make him happy? It's possible. I mean, what simpler way to have a child than to knock up somebody else's wife and not have to pay the kid's college tuition? Then again, maybe he would fight for paternity rights. Maybe the fact of a child would finally knock some commitment into the world's biggest commitment-phobe. Would he make room in his life for both me and a child? Is that what I want?

None of my questions gets answered, because, of course, he's not home when I phone. Probably surfing or lounging in the sun or sleeping with some gorgeous woman with perky breasts and adequate birth control. A few days later, he returns my call at work, while I'm in the resource room, and I send the three students who have shown up there for third period to the library. They walk out the door, and I know that there is no way any one of them will make it to the library, that all three will most likely wander the halls or go smoke in the bathroom or head out of the school building altogether and attempt to steal candy from the drugstore on the corner, but that is not my immediate concern.

What's going on? Ray says.

Not much.

Okay.

Except that I'm pregnant.

No, he says.

Yes, I say.

Well. Wow. Well. Congratulations, he says.

Thanks.

Wow. Another kid.

Guess so.

I thought you and Jim didn't sleep together.

Yeah, well, mostly we don't.

Okay, he says. If you say so.

End of July.

What's that?

That's when the baby's due. Tail end of July, beginning of August.

I'll mark my calendar.

If you count backwards, that means I got pregnant at the end of October.

[Silence]

Just about the same time as Melissa and Greg's wedding.

[Silence]

[Silence]

[Silence]

Oh, man, he says.

[Silence]

[Silence]

[Silence]

[Silence]

[Silence]

I don't know what to say, he says.

[Silence]

[Silence]

[Silence]

[Silence]

[Silence]

Jesus, he says.

[Silence]

No.

[Silence]

Just that once?

[Silence]

I doubt it.

[Silence]

I really, really doubt it.

[Silence]

I mean, that would be crazy, right?
[Silence]
Well, you're not going to have it, are you?
[Silence]
Julia?
Well, yeah, I'm going to have it.
[Silence]
[Silence]
Look. I'm going to have to call you back, all right?

12

I'm in the resource room, staring off into space, listening to the simultaneous conversations playing themselves over and over inside my brain, most of them lecturing me about my own idiocy, but several of them having the decency to stick up for me in my time of need, when Tina calls. She is sky-high with wedding plans.

I want you in the wedding, she says. I want you to be one of my bridesmaids.

Tina, I say. I'm honored, I really am. But think about it. By June, I will be huge. I'll be the big, fat pregnant blob. And you'll end up with a lifetime of people pointing at your wedding pictures and saying, Very nice, but who's the sumo wrestler in the pink dress?

You won't look like a sumo wrestler, she says. You'll look like a lovely pregnant woman.

I file this compliment away for later, when I might need it.

Besides, Tina says. The theme is cleavage, so you'll be perfect.

When someone says he'll call you back, what does that mean, exactly? Call you back in a couple of hours? Call you back that night? Call you back the next day when he's got a chunk of time to spare?

Clearly, none of these definitions is in Ray's dictionary. A week goes by and he does not call. Nor is there a message from him awaiting me in my e-mail inbox. I know this because I have checked my e-mail every half-hour or so for the last seven days. No, in Ray's world, saying you'll call someone back must mean something entirely different from what I take it to mean. Must mean next week or next month or next year. Might even mean never. Who knows?

I tell Elsa about waiting for the phone call from Ray, and she only half listens. She is in an atypically bad mood, her hair tied in a big mess on top of her head with a red and white scarf, her lips bare.

Did you hear me? I ask. We are in the teachers' lounge, surrounded by happy posters announcing upcoming happy events at the school that we will both happily skip, or at least walk out of at the earliest possible moment.

Elsa doesn't answer me.

What's wrong with you? I ask.

Nothing's wrong, she says.

She pours her coffee into the sink, runs the water, pours herself a new cup of coffee and drowns it with half-and-half. She opens three packets of Sweet'N Low at once and dumps them into her mug.

Claude gave me crabs, she says. All of that pretty pubic hair, crawling with crabs.

The news in my house is that Patricia has left her postman husband. My husband announces this tidbit over dinner one night as though it were an afterthought. As though we gossiped about people from the office all the time. As though Patricia were one of our regular topics of gossip.

She what? I ask.

Left her husband, Jim says.

We are sharing take-out Chinese food that Jim picked up on his way home from the office. For a couple of weeks now, this has been our routine. Dinner together a few nights a week. I've been wondering why.

Well, that's something, I say, not knowing what else to say.

I wait to hear more, wait to hear the part where Jim mentions how now that Patricia and the postman are splitsville, he and Patricia think they'd like to take a swing at the old relationship game. How he's only been waiting for Patricia to get her head on straight about the whole postman situation before following suit and leaving me. How he's sorry about the timing, what with me being knocked up and all, but hey, he never agreed to any of that anyway. But he doesn't say any of it. He simply returns to his chopsticks and his General Tso's chicken and says nothing further on the subject.

Jim seems to be coming around to the baby idea. Without saying anything, he digs around in the basement and emerges with the absurdly expensive French crib that we bought for Chad, and succeeds, after much swearing, in putting it back together. I am positive the crib harbors some awful child-safety infraction, being fifteen years old already, but I'm too relieved by Jim's actions to say anything. Next he dumps shoe boxes of old cassette tapes on the living room floor and pokes through them, looking for the kids' music that the two of us got way too used to listening to, the breaks and choruses as familiar as old Beatles tunes. He sets the tapes on a shelf in a neat row, ready for playing. He finds the boxes I haven't been able to part with, the ones filled with Chad's old barfed-on jammies and stained sweaters. He throws everything into the washing machine.

He ponders a lot. He stands staring at our glass coffee table with the sharp edges, evidently imagining scenarios involving bloody scalps and ambulances. He says things out of left field like: We'll have to fence the yard. Or: Have you seen my old mitt around? Or: Do you think you ought to be drinking that Diet Coke?

Bald Tom's new girlfriend is kaput. And this after he bought her some very expensive jewelry for Christmas and spent a romantic New Year's Eve with her at some fancy-shmancy hotel downtown, with champagne at midnight and room-service breakfast the next morning. Kaput. Gone. Decamped. Departed.

Tom can barely walk down the school hallway. I never noticed before, but he has awfully slumpy shoulders.

* * *

Ray keeps not calling. He is not going to call me back. This is all so typical and perfect. As if he would call me back! Of all the things I can count on in life, this is the most consistent: that when I need him most, Ray will not be there.

And then the phone rings and I break my cardinal rule of never picking up a ringing phone but instead waiting for the machine to pick it up just in case it turns out to be my mother, and find that, in fact, it is my mother. This is what rules are for, I remind myself. To save myself from just such a circumstance.

How are things? she asks, as though I might suddenly, after all these years, give her a truthful answer.

Gwen cannot believe that the second she retakes up smoking, I become unable to hang out in a smoke-filled environment.

Bad for the baby, I say. Doctor's orders.

Everything's conspiring against me, she says.

Gwen's husband and his receptionist have gone to the Virgin Islands together. This, after he's dragged Gwen and the kids on countless vacations to Civil War memorial parks. They are the only family I know of who have been to the Museum of American Presidents three times. He has a library of tapes of actors reading the Gettysburg Address and other momentous speeches from history.

We stand on Gwen's front porch so that she can smoke in peace.

You ever been to the Virgin Islands? she asks me.

I shake my head, even though, in truth, I have been to the Virgin Islands, for what now in retrospect seems to have been a happy week, years ago, with Jim.

Me neither, she says.

To my horror, Tina invites me to a pre-wedding gathering of the bridesmaids.

So that you can all get to know one another, she says. No presents or anything.

I can't help wondering if that's code for "Don't forget to bring a present." The wedding is already out of hand, what with showers and pre-showers and "get to know one another" parties months in advance, but I don't have the nerve to turn Tina down. Maybe this is normal these days. Maybe all brides-to-be throw dozens of pre-wedding events, all designed to help build excitement toward the big day.

The pre-wedding gathering of the bridesmaids takes place at the maid of honor's apartment. She turns out to be a heavy girl in a skinny girl's tank top, with a tattoo of a green dragon covering one shoulder.

Come in! she shouts, as if I were deaf.

Julia! Tina shouts.

Tina!

Get your butt in here!

All afternoon we shout. It seems to be an unwritten rule, right after "Wear a miracle bra, or don't show up." When we're not shouting, screaming is in order. Only after an hour and a half of eating, screaming, shouting, and drinking way too many pink cosmopolitans do we finally begin to calm down. Tina opens her presents with excruciating slowness, caressing each one like a newborn kitten before carefully loosening the gift wrap with her long, red-painted fingernails. I am ready to jump out of my skin. Did everyone shop at the same lingerie store? When the boxes are all opened, Tina is left with nothing but a tiny pile of teensy-weensy underthings, each uncomfortable-looking in its own unique way. She gazes around the room at her friends. When she starts to speak, it is in subdued tones, and everyone hushes to listen.

I just want to say, she says. I just want to say how blessed I feel to have all of you here with me today. It means so much to me. Thank you.

Light murmurs all around.

And especially, Tina says, especially I'd like to thank my sister-in-law, Julia, for putting up with my brother and my family and for being a part of all of this, even though she's obviously not feeling all that well today, being pregnant and all. Love you, Julia!

I look at Tina and see that her eyes are wet and glowing. And then the room falls silent. There's an expectancy in the atmosphere, although it takes me a good long beat to realize that what is expected is for me to say something in return. All the other bridesmaids look at me with colossal, amazingly real, albeit half-drunk, smiles. Tina too. She looks ready to implode with emotion.

Love you too, Tina! I shout. Or at least I try to shout. What with the big rock that seems to have lodged in my throat, the words pretty much choke their way into the room, where they are greeted with a warm round of applause.

I worry about my mothering skills. I think I'm lacking in certain areas. I never was a mother who played games, for instance. Lord knows, I tried. Lord knows, I bought all the games known to modern man, stacked them on the officially designated game shelf in the family room, read the instructions, shuffled the cards, unfolded the boards, set out the pieces. But the actual playing of the games never struck me as anything less than torture. And I could never fake it. Could never pretend I was having a swell time collecting that bucket of plastic cherries, or trying to trap the mouse, or picking the ranch house in The Game of Life.

How many games of fish can a person play? How often can you topple a Jenga tower and still find it hilarious?

On the other hand, I have always been the kind of mother ready to spring for a double-scoop ice cream cone with sprinkles or a plate of french fries in the middle of the afternoon, or an extralarge bucket of popcorn and a package of Junior Mints at the movies. That should count for something, shouldn't it?

I am deep into morning sickness the day Jim takes Chad and me to the pound to look for a dog. There is no arguing with him about it. He's decided we need a dog to round out the family.

You'll like it, he says, more of a command than a suggestion.

I take it as a good sign. I take it as Jim's belief that all of this will work out neatly in the end. And if he can believe it, I can believe it, too. A husband, a couple of kids, a dog, a house in the suburbs: What more could I possibly want? It requires all my willpower, but I don't allow myself to dwell on the answer.

Jim drives, and Chad sits in the backseat, and I have to admit to being slightly hepped by the idea of rescuing an animal from the jaws of death. Surely this is good for some points with the Big Man upstairs, I tell myself. Surely this bodes well for a hyperhealthy, genius-IQ'd baby in my near future. A baby with no need to know for certain about its parentage.

The pound, not improbably, stinks like nobody's business, but the noise level wins by a knockout. The prisoners bark with desperation, their unanswered calls bouncing off the concrete walls in a form of unknowing self-torture. Barks begetting more barks, begetting more barks, begetting more barks, ad nauseam. I could throw an epileptic fit in the middle of the floor, or do my rendition of the final lines of "Climb Ev'ry Mountain" and no one would hear me.

Jim and Chad stroll the aisles, casually remarking on the occupants. How bad is it that the two of them remind me of Nazis, coolly deciding the fate of living things? The dogs are a sad lot: old, misshapen, shaggy, crippled, over-sized, undersized, legs too short, ears too cropped, tails too bushy—you name it. The pound has a nondiscrimination policy. And of course, each old, misshapen creature takes a hold of your heart and squeezes until you can't breathe, can't hear, can't speak. I'm ready to take them all home, the whole lot of them. By the time we finish making the rounds, I'm a basket case of emotion.

Fortunately, my Nazi companions are more collected.

Didn't see anything, Jim says.

Me neither, Chad says. Let's check out the puppy room.

I will agree on no other puppy in the place than the last of the black ones, all alone in his vast lonely cell. He is the outcast of the group, left to suffer in silence, his cuter, peppier brother snatched up moments before by an aging, ponytailed hippie and his aging hippie wife. This last puppy is frozen in fear. A dinky, moaning mass of short black fur.

Jim wants one of the brown pups that are busy climbing over one another in happy community. He plucks one from the group, and the little guy goes nuts, scratching and licking at him merrily.

Here, Jim says.

But I won't budge. It's the lonely guy or no one.

When we get him home, he sits on my feet for several hours before peeing on the rug.

Sparky, I call him.

Mystery solved: Patricia has moved in with Brad.

Been sleeping with him for weeks now, Jim says.

Brad? I ask.

Yeah.

Brad-from-your-office Brad?

Yeah.

Wow, I say. That's really something.

Jim doesn't say anything.

Fucking Brad, I say to myself, just to hear the sound of the words on my lips.

Somehow, it falls on me to train the puppy. As though I had the slightest idea how to accomplish such a thing. As though I had asked for a dog in the first place. As though I weren't feeling sick as a dog myself.

After consulting a few books on the subject, I come up with a routine. I strap the little doggy leash to Sparky's little doggy collar, and together we make a few rounds of the yard, me waiting on Sparky to poop on the grass, Sparky seeing how long he can go without pooping. This while I stand half stooped in the damp cold, stomach churning. I never imagined how happy I'd be to see a dog take a shit on my own front lawn.

I tell myself that it doesn't matter who the father is, really. I mean, millions of kids are adopted all the time, and they don't have a clue who their fathers are, right? *Or* their mothers. And they grow up to be just fine, don't they? They grow up to be bank presidents, or lawyers, or heads of multinational corporations, don't they? And then think of all of those children who *do* know who their parents are. A vast number of them are completely fucked up, am I right? So since when does parentage really matter all that much, as long as you have a loving home in which to grow up? I don't let myself ponder the loving-home part for long. Nor do I dwell on the fact that my baby isn't anything like an adopted child, but is instead being deprived merely of the truthfulness of his paternity. Still, the whole thing gets to me, until at last I must kick Sparky off my feet and waste a few hours seeing what items of clothing I can still squeeze into.

I miss my Klonopins. I used to wonder what life would be like without Klonopin. Now I know. Life sucks without Klonopin. Life is really, really stark without Klonopin, like getting cable after all the years of fucking around with an antenna. Things look really up-close-and-personal. And there's no break from it. The clarity keeps shining through, day after day, one long, relentless march of sharp-edged reality.

And I don't want to see my therapist anymore if Klonopin isn't the prize for seeing him, like getting a lollipop after a shot. What is the point of all that talking if the chemicals in my brain won't sit down and behave? They're like bad teenagers, listening to loud music and smashing the furniture and waking up with a train wreck of a hangover. You can't make them all at once pay attention, even if what they're supposed to be paying attention to is their own stupid thoughts. Chaos, that's what they call it.

However, for you, little alien unit, I remain Klonopin-free.

Drunk Ray finally calls, about a century too late. I have to admit, there's something endearing about Drunk Ray, bad as that might sound. Drunk Ray has no edges. Drunk Ray says stupid things. Drunk Ray says what Regular Ray might say if Regular Ray weren't so fucking inhibited.

This time Drunk Ray says, I love you. He says, It's not my baby, right? He says, When are you going to leave that guy, anyway?

Drunk Ray wouldn't be so bad, if only he weren't so loaded.

The baby's not yours, Ray, I tell him. So don't worry about it.

13

My obstetrician is a bit too young and perky, but I continue to see her, since at this point in life showing my vagina to new people is no longer my cup of tea. I figure this doctor's viewed my whole wide-open deal in explicit, living, fully lit-up color already. No great shock to her system. She's poked around my body while carrying on one inane conversation or another, so natural at it that sometimes I picture her shock at finding that while she was chatting away her hands had somehow crept up my vagina. And she's sweet as can be, excessively petite, with a nose you might expect to see on a five-year-old—barely a bump on the smooth surface of her face.

Laura is her name. That's what I'm supposed to call her. Plain Laura. Although it makes me slightly uncomfortable, this first-name familiarity.

Looks good! is what Laura tells me every appointment, after a good look-see at my nearly naked body.

I'd pay twice the price just for the pleasure of hearing those words.

Relationship Test #4:

There is a bee in the house. You don't know how it got there, but that isn't the issue. The fact is, it's there, buzzing from room to room. You ask your husband to get rid of the bee. He tells you you're a big girl, get rid of it yourself. You tell him that bees are not in your line of experience. He shakes his head, says the bee isn't bothering him, goes back to whatever it is he was doing. You ask him, Please. You tell him there's a blow job waiting for him in this one. You tell him a decent blow job, not one that ends before the final curtain, but the real thing, from start to end. Your husband rises, rolls up a magazine, and knocks the bee to kingdom come.

Afterward, you:

A. Tell him you were kidding, of course. What was he thinking?

B. Laugh at him for thinking you could possibly be serious.

C. Berate him for killing the bee instead of honorably transferring it outside, thereby canceling the blow-job deal.

I don't remember feeling this sick when I was pregnant with Chad. Fourteen weeks and counting, and I'm still sick to my stomach. I'm kind of proud of the little alien—no bigger than a thumb and already able to bring its big, fat mommy to her knees.

Stacy says that means this one is a girl. Stacy tells me that being sick is a good sign. That the sicker the mother, the prettier the baby. Something about the baby sucking all of the good stuff right out of you—all of the beauty and good health. I don't know how Stacy knows this, seeing as how she is childless. But that's Stacy for you—full of unanticipated morsels.

But I'm just plain sick of being sick. It's tedious. Cosmic Pregnant Lady no longer senses the beauty in the natural flow of things. Finding a bit of barf in your hair hours after barfing will do that to you.

Stacy says that a friend of hers was sick the whole nine months, right up until her due date. Spent a good six months of it in bed, sucking on crackers.

And you should see her kid now, Stacy says. Six-foot-four, plays on the football team. Eagle Scout. Four-point student.

I consider throwing up on Stacy and making it seem like an accident, but decide against it.

I'm not altogether certain that Chad lives with us anymore. Things move, food gets eaten, toilets flush at odd hours, dollar bills disappear from my wallet at regular intervals, so I suppose that technically he hasn't moved out and forgotten to leave a forwarding address. But he is remarkably out of sight during all those moments when you might most expect to see him, like anytime during the day, for example.

Giving motherhood a second try makes me well aware of my failures the first time around. Because of this, and because I'm as much of a snoop as anybody else, and because I can't remember the last time I set foot into Chad's bedroom to see what he had hanging on his walls, I decide to take a peek inside. You've probably read those newspaper articles about teenagers who build bombs in their rooms or run drug enterprises from their desks or harbor caches of firearms under their beds and the parents don't even know about it. I am one of those parents. For all I know, Chad could be smuggling nuclear secrets to China.

I knock a few hundred times first. I call out Chad's name through the door.

Honey! I yell. Are you in there?

I finally open the door. I don't find any nuclear secrets, gun caches, or drug paraphernalia, unless you count the hash pipe, which I don't. What I do find is an ocean of clothing and books and CDs, and a smell strong enough to wake the dead—testosterone and intense B.O. and several other reeking scents the origin of which I have no desire to contemplate.

I open the drawer of the nightstand. There isn't much there. A roll of deodorant. An old bottle of stinky cologne. A rusting nail clipper. I pull out a small spiral notebook and strum through the pages. Empty. Totally empty. The internal life of Chad remains a mystery.

I leave him a note on the kitchen table in order to make contact. "Chad-Man," I write—the nickname bestowed on him in newborn testicular glory—"are you still with us? If so, an indication might be nice."

The next morning, he surprises me with a fat kiss on the cheek.

Ma, he says. How goes it?

You never know. That should be written on a little card attached to a headpiece that sits in front of my forehead so that I can read it over and over as the days progress, and never, ever forget its message. Because the thing is, most of the time you think that you *do* know, or that you mostly know, when in fact you never do.

The thing that, most recently, I didn't know is that Elsa has a daughter. And not just any daughter but a daughter who was born with no muscle tone whatsoever and a toothpick-slim chance of survival. A totally disabled child. She had this daughter, Lilly, a year after marrying Claude, and they gave her up right then and there, in the hospital. When they came home, they painted over the nursery and Claude drove all the baby things to Goodwill. Elsa never got pregnant again.

This is something she lives with, day after day.

And now she's left Claude. The crab thing put her over the edge.

To think I once shaved my vulva for that motherfucker, she says.

My mother calls to say she has a lot of mucus in her throat and do I ever have that same problem—a lot of mucus in the neck region, ready to be coughed up and spit into a handkerchief? She says this to a pregnant lady, mind you. Someone who gags at the mere thought of a handkerchief's purpose in life, much less its graphic use.

I'm sorry to hear that, I tell her.

[Little choking noises and a surge of throat clearing]

Gwen appears at my doorstep in a brown terry-cloth robe, hair wrapped in a scarf, mascara smeared, a cigarette in one hand and a martini glass in the other. She looks like an aging movie star between takes. Did anyone mention that it is three in the morning?

He called, she says. He wants to come back.

No.

Yes.

What are you going to do?

I don't know, she says. She taps the ash from her cigarette into the fireplace, and I pull at the hem of the old T-shirt I'm wearing in a valiant attempt to cover my bare butt.

Get drunk, I guess, she says.

Jim comes downstairs in his boxers, holding his arms across his bare, hairy chest.

What's going on? he asks.

Bill wants Gwen to let him come back.

Christ, he says.

Gwen starts to cry into her martini and Jim reaches his pasty, naked arms out to her and I give up trying to cover my butt and I reach out for her also, exposing the vast moons of my pink butt cheeks to the air, and in that mo-

ment Chad decides to materialize from out of nowhere—
Chad, whom we've barely seen since Christmas.

Chad, I say.

Mom, he says.

Gwen just dropped by.

Chad takes a long, narrow-eyed, sarcastic drink of the situation.

Whatever, he says, and disappears into the hallway.

Jim paints the baby's room lavender, which he claims is a good color either way. He buys new baby blankets and a new lavender bumper for the crib, one without frills. He sets a row of little stuffed bears across the top of the new baby dresser, and then stands back to admire it. He's like a brand-new gay guy, fresh out of the closet, all atwitter with fabrics and colors. He wants to paint green vines and bulging grapes around the room's edges. He wants to paint clouds on the baby's ceiling.

He never mentions Patricia anymore.

Just when I can afford no further mental challenges to my exhausted brain without bursting, I find several drops of dark blood in my underwear.

My perky obstetrician says there is probably nothing to worry about. A bit of spotting can be perfectly normal. But can I come in to see her? Today? Right now?

Jim meets me at the clinic. He is breathless. He wants me to sit down, stop moving, stop talking, stop doing anything that might make matters worse. He says over and over, I'm sure this is normal. I'm sure everything's fine. He asks the receptionist how much longer it's going to be. He whips through an ancient, mangled *Sports Illustrated* that somehow made its way into the pile of *Good Housekeeping*s and *People*s and *Shape*s. He asks the receptionist how much longer it's going to be. He gets a drink of water in a miniature cone-shaped paper cup from the water dispenser next to the fish tank. He stares into the fish tank. He doesn't like the fish in the fish tank. He doesn't like the chairs, they're not deep enough. He doesn't like the lighting. He doesn't like the carpeting. He really, really, really does not like the receptionist. He asks her how much longer it's going to be. Let me check for you, she says, then disappears.

Chad was a perfect baby. Slept through the night, hardly cried, healthy and content. From there, things went downhill. So I'm hoping that the alien unit is merely doing the opposite. Scaring me shitless now in exchange for a lifetime of calm.

Laura arrives, and Jim is horrified at the sight of her.

How old is she? he whispers, as we follow her down the hallway to the ultrasound room. Fifteen?

I don't bother to answer. If there is one person among the three of us with the right to speak in panicky tones, I think most of the modern world, given a chance, would grant that right to me. I try not to waste any energy getting pissed at Jim. The little unit needs all my heartbeats right now.

I lie down on the cot, and Laura squirts some gunk on my belly and then rubs the gunk around with the thinga-mabob, which somehow manages to look through my fat and skin and membranes to find the little alien, hanging out in fluid, taking its little alien swim. I find this more than incredible—that beyond the weirdness of the penis-vagina union, and the sperm swimmers doing an Olympic sprint for an ovum, and all of that wild cell division that eventually forms a human, that there were, once upon a time, for every one of us, several months when we swam in our own miniature sea, tiny fish taking in mouthfuls of water, with air the enemy rather than a necessity.

We all watch the alien relaxing in its murky den. How sweet it looks in there. A tiny person with a big head on top of its neck right where I'd been hoping to find it, and arms and legs in all the right places. The doctor snaps a picture.

Hey you, I say to the swimmer. Hang in there.

* * *

Apparently, nothing to worry about. Apparently, just one of those things. One of those percentage things where some women bleed and some women don't and there really are times when there isn't any rhyme or reason to the whole thing, or if there is a reason, we don't know what it is yet. So. There you have it. No big deal. Go back to work.

Elsa is miserable. She sits across from me at the diner, downing an entire plate of french fries covered in salt, tossing back about fifty cups of coffee. She's makeup-less. Her eyes lack their usual presence, her lips look small and thin. She's more like a relative of herself than the real thing, a depressed twin sister, her luggage lost at the airport so that now she is forced to dress in Elsa's crazy attire. There is an overwhelming matronly quality to her—a middle-aged, heavy-bosomed woman in what looks like a Girl Scout uniform.

I can't eat, she says.

You just ate a plate of fries.

You know what I mean.

And I do know what she means. I say to her, What are you going to do?

Oh, eventually I'll go back to Claude, she says. I always do.

And then Chad gets back together with Tricia. Not that he reveals this piece of information to me himself. But running into shirtless Tricia at two in the morning in the hallway is a bit of a clue. She looks fabulous and young, her skin taut and fresh, her face flushed with embarrassment as she tries to cover herself with her thin white arms.

I am floored at the sight of her. Not that she is here, in my hallway, half naked while Chad awaits her return in his bedroom a few feet away. That part is a given. No, what floors me is Tricia's youth. Her simplicity. Her utter innocence at the same moment she thinks herself full of nerve. What I want to say is, You are beautiful. What I want to tell her is that one day her lovely heart will be shattered in pieces. What I want to do is save her from all the shit that lies ahead. Let her know that life is one long march through closing doors, that she should be sure to choose hers wisely. But of course, I don't say any of it. Hey, is what I say.

Hey, Tricia.

* * *

My mother: You couldn't tell me you were bleeding?

Me: Ma. It's all right. It was nothing.

My mother: I'm the last to know. You'd think you'd call and tell me.

She's not the last to know. Ray is. I can't stop myself from calling him. Looking at the phone and not calling Ray is like being really hungry in front of a bowl of potato chips. Eventually you're going to eat them.

He's not home. I get his answering machine, and because I haven't planned what to say in the event of his answering machine, I actually do the smart thing and hang up before saying something really stupid that I can't erase. Then I call again and leave a stupid message.

Ray, I say. It's me. Had a bit of a scare recently but apparently everything's all right. With the baby. Okay, then. Just thought I'd let you know.

I hang up the phone and want to kill myself. And then Ray doesn't call back and I really want to kill myself. My learning curve has no vertical motion. Flat as a corpse and nearly as unresponsive.

* * *

I am also ready to murder little Sparky. I am certain that terrible things await me in the afterlife for harboring such terrible thoughts about probably the sweetest dog in the universe. But I can't help it. Sparky is just more than I can handle. He has chewed through everything. He has pawed great gashes in all the doors. He has peed in every corner. He has shed on every square inch of the house. He refuses to keep to the borders of our yard, and insists on scaring the wits out of me by repeatedly running the two blocks it takes to reach the busy thoroughfare. I chase him the best I can, call his name, plead with him to come. But no. He wants to run between cars. He wants to shit on the unfriendly neighbor's lawn. He wants to throw up on the carpet in the middle of the night. He wants to be fed, to be petted, to go out, to come in, to bark, bark, bark, bark, bark, bark, bark, at a bird, a car, the UPS man, the damn nameless cat that prowls our yard. I fantasize about ways to knock him off without anyone being the wiser. Poison looms large. I pray for one of those doggy diseases that everybody else's dog seems to get. I hope for an accident that isn't my fault. I feel terrible about having these thoughts—especially when Sparky looks at me with his big black eyes, or sets his little head on my feet to rest—but I can't stop the mental carnage.

* * *

My therapist shaves his mustache. I ask you: Is that right? Is that fair? Is he allowed to change his appearance so that every time I look at him I have to remind myself that he is, in fact, the very same person to whom I have entrusted the embarrassing intimate details of my sorry little life? It's depressing, that something so stable should suddenly change. I'd grown fond of that mustache without realizing it, the white hairs pressed lovingly over his top lip. Now his barren lip lies across the bottom half of his face, exposed, pale, thin. He looked better before. Do I tell him this?

Bad omens everywhere. I am sitting in the grocery store parking lot, my car idling, waiting for a spot to open up. It seems safe enough. After all, I am not in motion, I am not talking to anyone I might unknowingly offend, I am not speaking on the phone to my mother, I am not in a high-crime neighborhood, I am not doing much of anything beyond breathing and taking up otherwise unoccupied space in this universe. No, it is a moment of unexpected nothingness, just me and my car radio and the possibility of future movement. It is, in its own way, a moment of pleasure. And then someone hits my car. I watch it happen, watch the green car back up when it should not be backing up, watch it approach, watch my hand fly to the horn and press. A slight crunch ensues. My bumper caves

Mary Guterson

in. And in the next moment, the green car is pulling away and I am aware of the fact that just as I am telling myself to get the license-plate number, or at least the make of the car, or if nothing else, a good look at the asshole who just punched in my bumper, I am completely and utterly without the ability to do so. I am a useless witness to the crime. All I take note of—and as I take note of it I'm aware that this is the most easily removed piece of evidence in the world—all I can remember with any strong certainty besides the car's being green, is a bumper sticker on its rear end. "I'm with the Band," it says.

My mother: You're starting to get fat, dear.

Me: I'm pregnant, Mother.

My mother: Of course, you're pregnant. That's no reason to let yourself go.

And then shit happens, as it always does.

14

My doctor is unavailable. I'm bleeding again and my doctor is nowhere in sight. This is not good. Doctors are supposed to be available for emergencies. That's what we pay them for. It's a contract: We pay them thousands and thousands of dollars, and they promise to be there when something goes haywire. Bleeding, for instance. Freaking out, for another. But because my doctor is currently not available to hear me freak out, I must wait for the doctor-partner, a man I've met only once and then only briefly, as a mere formality—an introduction in case of the impossible circumstance of my own doctor's being unavailable for the alien's entrance. A man I hardly glanced at before winking at my perky obstetrician and shoving playfully at her arm, saying, You'll be there for me, right? You won't miss this one, will you? Big laughs all around, my perky gal nodding along and winking right back and saying, Not for the world.

But apparently she wasn't talking about early arrivals. And this one is way too early. I'm barely nineteen weeks.

Well, well. There is an underground tunnel that leads from my obstetrician's office to the hospital. Who knew? The doctor-partner says I shouldn't walk, and so I get a wheel-chair ride through the narrow hallways, pushed by an orderly whose name I didn't catch, as my mind has just now gone blank with fear. The doctor-partner has told me nothing except that he doesn't know what is happening, better for me to be at the hospital in case something needs to be done. And I'm too wiped out to form the questions I'm sure I should be asking. Questions like: What the fuck is going on?

I am thrust into a *Star Trek* episode. I am beamed up to the fourth floor, where nurses in white uniforms cruise past and orderlies pushing strange-looking contraptions on silver carts rush by and phones ring and lights flash and buzzers buzz and elevator doors shush open to reveal the latest beamed-up arrival. It's another world on the fourth floor. I am rolled past doors and desks and a wall of abandoned IV poles. I pass a woman in a loose hospital gown, her feet swaddled in enormous furry blue slippers. The woman is taking her IV pole for a walk. And then a nurse carrying a tiny bundled-up baby. And then a door with a huge bundle of blue balloons. And laughter. And by the time I am finally released into the silence of room 417, it dawns on me where I am. The baby floor.

For a while, nothing. I'm left to my own devices in the stark privacy of room 417. The orderly who dropped me here has disappeared without saying good-bye. I've no clue what I'm supposed to be doing. I concentrate on not bleeding. Happy families pass by my door, their voices clapping through my ears and then quickly fading to nothingness. Everyone else seems to have a purpose. Visitor, patient, baby. I'm all three at once.

I try to make myself useful. I test the volume control on the television set. I flush the toilet and find it in good working order. I stare at myself very closely in the mirror and find a pimple embedded in the valley next to my left nostril, and because I am now looking for signs from God, I decide that the appearance of this pimple is not a good sign. I swear at it. Finally, I creep slowly to the nurses' station and ask what it is exactly they'd like for me to do. I'm pretty much holding my breath now. The nurse looks up at me from behind a pair of speckle-framed reading glasses. She is clearly not happy to be interrupted. Not a good sign.

What room are you? she asks.

Four seventeen.

She stabs at her computer keyboard, studies the information on the screen. Does something pass through her eyes?

You'll need to put on a gown and get in bed, she says. They don't want you walking.

Definitely not a good sign.

Jim arrives, looking ashen. He flips through the TV channels a few hundred times. He reads the patient menu. His leg shakes up and down viciously, like the needle on a sewing machine. He gets up, looks out the door, comes back and sits again. He flips through the channels some more, settles on a foreign soccer game. The players kick the ball up and down the field, knock it with their heads. He flips off the television.

How you doing? he asks.

I shake my head.

He leans over to kiss me, then takes both my hands in his.

Everything's going to be all right, he says.

Okay, I say.

He makes a couple of phone calls to work. He rustles

through the newspaper. He uses the bathroom, washes up at the sink, pours us both water to drink, looks out the window. He walks to the door, looks up and down the hall, and then sits again. I know he's upset and jumpy and nervous and he could probably use some comforting himself. Trouble is, I haven't got the capacity for it at the moment. Not when I'm trying to comfort the alien already.

No offense, I tell him, finally. But you're driving me crazy.

Jim goes back to the office, and although I really did want him to go, now I am lonely. It doesn't help that dozens of families are celebrating the happy births of healthy babies up and down the hallway. I'm the single holdout. No happy births in room 417. Not today, anyway. I concentrate on not bleeding again.

I consider calling Gwen but change my mind. Gwen would only get all weepy and nervous, and I've cornered the weepy/nervous department. Elsa would come in a snap, but I don't really want to see her right now, either. I don't want to see anybody. I don't want to be lonely, but I don't want to be with anyone. I am truly fucked up.

Then I remember I've still got the alien for company.

You and me, babe, I tell it.

* * *

I may as well have disappeared down a black hole. No one seems to know who I am or what I am doing here. I am the invisible patient. The ghost of 417. The doctor never arrives to check on me. Instead, a series of nurses come to take my temperature, over and over, and then my blood pressure, and every so often a new guy shows up to take blood from my arm. It is by far the most exhausting thing in the world—going to a hospital to rest. I can feel the alien getting antsy and fed up. I can feel the alien thinking, I can't take much more of this.

It occurs to me that the alien is stronger than I am. It will do whatever its little alien mind wants. I have no control here. I can't make it clean its room or do its homework. I can't make it happy. For Christ's sake, I can't make it breathe air.

Every time I go to the bathroom there is blood, so I decide to not go to the bathroom anymore. I'm not going to let the little alien slip out without a fight.

I quit drinking water. I decide not to move. I close my eyes and attempt to empty my brain of thoughts. I fail utterly.

* * *

It grows dark outside my window. Suddenly it is night. I don't know where the time has gone. It has disappeared in a series of nurses and ringing phones, an orderly refilling the paper towels, someone checking on my water pitcher, someone else asking me questions.

A new nurse arrives, heavy and damp-looking. She has a mammoth chest. She smells like peppermint. She gives my chart a brief scan and then tells me to drink some water. Not good to get dehydrated. Something about her demeanor makes me listen. She seems the only person around who actually sees me.

I feel about six years old, sipping at my paper cup while the heavy nurse waits to refill it.

One more, she says. There you go. All of it.

Later she accompanies me to the toilet, waits for me to pee, and then checks to see what's been produced. Where do these people come from? Those willing to poke through the bloody masses emitted from another human's body.

She walks me back to the bed and helps me sit. Then she does the unexpected. She sits down next to me. It makes no sense, but it's a great comfort having her there, with her big body smelling of peppermint. She doesn't move. She's got all the time in the world. I can hear her breathing. It seems the most compassionate of acts—this woman's willingness to sit beside me and just breathe, quietly. She's a sign, there's no doubt about it. A big one.

I'm going to lose it, aren't I? I finally ask.

She looks at me. It's clear she's not supposed to say. Probably could get sued for telling the truth.

Yes, she says. Yes, you are.

The next thing I know, I am weeping in her big arms. And then the nurse is gone, out the door, her message delivered, and I don't see her again.

It happens a while later, right there in room 417. And because the nurse has told me it will happen, I am no longer afraid. The doctor-partner tells me to push, and so I push the alien out, and lo and behold, it's not an alien at all but a teeny, tiny exquisite human child. A girl. Bald. Translucent. Perfect. A princess of a girl, with ten amazingly perfect fingers and ten incredibly miniature toes, her wee legs folded like a pretzel, her arms spread wide. She's no bigger than my palm.

Someone places her in a stainless-steel bowl and leaves her on the tray table. And because the world I now inhabit bears no resemblance to the other one I used to live in, the one where I was fat and pregnant and life seemed to offer a whole new future, this fact seems only one more new weirdness to accept—the fact of my baby in a bowl. The little thing is lying on her side, cleverly assuming the fetal position, left ear up. Her skin couldn't be more than a single layer thick. I'm afraid to touch her. I'm afraid my touch might hurt her. And that's when I see it. At the tip of her ear a tiny chunk is missing. I have the exact same chunk missing from my own left ear. The sight of it kills me.

I love her like there's no tomorrow. And for her, there isn't.

15

Carl. That's what the doctor-partner's name turns out to be. Carl. He comes to see me first thing in the morning. He looks wide awake. He's wearing regular clothes, a pair of khakis, a button-down shirt. If you saw him on the street, you'd have no idea he spends his days staring down women's vaginas, watching baby humans slide into the atmosphere. You'd have no idea the carnage he must sometimes witness. The accidents. The alien births. You might be standing in line behind him at the grocery store checkout, waiting to pay for a loaf of bread, mere hours after he's placed somebody's dead baby in a stainless-steel bowl for safekeeping. He sits in a chair next to my bed and asks how I'm doing. I can only shrug. It's all I've got left in my repertoire of responses. It's been a long night.

Carl purses his lips. He tells me these things sometimes happen. He tells me there's no one to blame. He tells me there's no reason not to give it another try. Three or four months from now.

I'm too wasted to answer. It seems such a crazy suggestion, like telling me it's not too late to become a professional ice skater. I wanted one baby, and that was the alien. I'm not about to create another.

A bit later, Jim arrives. The bowl is in the bathroom on the shelf where I've left it. Together we stare at her for a while. Jim doesn't cry. He's clinical in his assessment of her. He's fascinated, the way you'd be with a curious lab specimen. He looks at her closely. Examines her.

That's incredible, he says.

We are sitting together in silence—me on the bed, Jim in the chair—when a nurse arrives. A young thing I haven't seen before.

Okay, she says.

We both look at her.

Okay, she says. I've got to take it now. To the lab.

I hadn't really thought about this part. I had forgotten that the future still arrives. That something would have to happen next. That we couldn't spend the next week checking on the progress of the dead baby in the bowl.

Next thing you know, the nurse has whisked her waif-like self into the bathroom. A half-second later she emerges, failing in her attempt to hide in the crook of her elbow the bowl that holds the baby. Then she darts out of the room, a stream of cool air in her wake. That's it. That's all she wrote. The alien, she is gone.

Conversation number one:

My mother: You know, I never had a miscarriage.

Conversation number two:

My mother: It's a good thing you got that dog.

If you look for the silver lining, you can sometimes convolute things enough to find one. Like the fact that it is impossible to speak without crying after you've seen your own dead baby in a stainless-steel bowl. Because if you were, in fact, able to speak, you might find yourself saying "Fuck off" a few million times to all the well-meaning people who suddenly appear at the door or on the phone or who send you a card in the mail, telling you that it's probably all for the best in some unknown way, that God knows what he's doing, that you were chosen, that it's an honor to carry such a perfect spirit if even for such a short time, that you were getting old anyway, that you still have Chad, that you still have your health, that you still have so much to be thankful for, that you are strong and healthy and vital and fertile, that God hasn't seen the end of you yet! To all of this and more, you would have to shout "Fuck off," if, in fact, you weren't so completely unable to form words or thoughts or motions. If you were able to, say, get off of the couch. There's a silver lining in there somewhere, goddammit, you just have to look for it.

The perky obstetrician never calls. You'd think she'd have a moment in her perky life to call her formerly pregnant patient and say something deep and perkily meaningful. You'd think she'd at least leave a phone message. But no. She never does.

Ray doesn't call, either, not that he'd have any reason to. He's a selfish bastard, that one. I've spent half a life loving a selfish bastard.

Chad doesn't say much, simply plunks himself down

in a chair across from me and sits there, looking very grown up. The fact that he, too, is sad just kills me, and it's made worse by the fact that I am too wiped out to properly acknowledge his sadness. Every once in a while he offers to bring me something, or else he goes ahead and brings me something without asking. He's a pretty good mind-reader. Like handing me a glass of orange juice before I even know I'm thirsty. Or telling someone on the phone that I'm not available right now, when I'm nothing if not available. He's a good guy.

Jim, too. He slowly dismantles the baby's bedroom in a way that he hopes is covert. He paints over the grape-vines and the clouds on the ceiling. He puts a desk where the crib used to be. He sets a pair of bookshelves next to the desk, fills them with books on baseball. He cooks din-ners and opens bottles of wine. Now and then he sets a hand on my head and holds it there.

The two of them play Scrabble into the night, keeping me company while I sit on the couch, half listening.

Sparky sits on my feet all day. It's brutal, how much that stupid dog loves me. If I pick up his leash, the dog goes apeshit with delirium, anticipating a stroll around the neighborhood. You'd think he'd just won the lottery. It's an amazing thing, how little it takes to make him happy. Half a doggy biscuit. A walk to the mailbox. A bird on the lawn. A pair of stinky feet to lie on.

* * *

Momentary truisms:

1. When you are utterly exhausted and spent, you will find it impossible to sleep.

2. Sleeping pills are God's gift to the utterly exhausted and spent.

Here is the way to make it through the endless hours that constitute a day: First, you stay in bed as long as possible. On a good day, this can take up nearly all the daylight hours. But most of the time, you'll sooner or later have to get out of bed, if only to use the bathroom. A few subsequent hours can be spent sitting on the couch, staring off into space. Making cups of coffee uses up minutes, even more if you fill the kettle to the brim so that it takes longer for the water to boil. And because coffee in your cup goes cold so quickly, you can make several cups before you are sick of waiting for water to boil. Then it's time for a shower. You stand under the hot water until there is no more hot water. Emerge. Dry off. Put on robe. Wait for hair to dry. Wait for more hot water. Repeat. There is the endless fun of flipping through the television channels, particularly the Christian channels where women with big hair and globs of eye makeup go orgasmic for God and money. You might ponder such a career for a while, before finding a rerun of The Love Boat on another channel. Darkness arrives. Have you eaten? Hard to say. Does a bite of a Snickers bar qualify as eating? The countdown begins toward the time when it's safe to swallow another sleeping pill. Waste a few minutes studying the veins in your thighs. Throw out old underwear. Find tissues in the bottom of your bed. Cry. Ignore the phone. Take your pill. Sleep like a baby.

16

I use up my two personal days and all my remaining sick leave, and then it's time to return to the resource room. Things look different. Someone has sharpened about a zillion No. 2 pencils and placed them inside of a red pencil holder on top of my desk. My bulletin board has been relieved of old notices and outdated calendars. My files are pristine, the bookshelves organized by subject matter. The candy wrappers in my desk drawers have been disposed of, replaced by fresh reams of paper and blue pens. My computer screen is miraculously wiped clean of fingerprints and dust; the keyboard looks new.

And the kids. They sit quietly at their desks with open

books. No one asks to use the bathroom. No one drops Doritos on the floor. No one steals my printer cartridge.

It's fucking eerie. I've half a mind to light up a cigarette and set off the smoke alarm just to jump-start things back to normal.

I look at the board. In the space reserved for my Word of the Day, someone has written: "You. We're all thinking about you."

Elsa takes me to the diner for lunch. She orders, and even though I don't hear what she orders, I say I'll have the same.

There's nothing a person can say, Elsa tells me.

I know.

There's no language for it, she says.

I nod. I'd forgotten about Elsa's baby, the one she left in the hospital. I'd forgotten this painful piece of Elsa's existence.

I never got over it, she says. Ever.

Tom is so sweet I almost wish I could work up a crush on him again. He is smart enough to not say a word, just comes into the resource room and hugs me, right there, in front of the kids, who are in that moment smart enough not to smirk or make rude comments. Everybody is walking on eggshells around me. Tom is a tight hugger, one hand around the back of my head, holding me to his shoulder. He smells of shaving cream. He breathes in and out a few times. He is transferring something to me through his touch, a Tom message, and I receive it.

I spend a lot of afternoons at Gwen's, smoking. We have mastered the fine art of speaking volumes by merely uttering the word "fuck." We have entire conversations made up of this single syllable separated by long silences, deep breaths, head shakings, cigarettes, coffee, pieces of pound cake. Fuck.

The world is suddenly filled with pregnant women. There they are, knocked up right and left. Big fat mamas with big fat bellies and their big-mama Suburbans, soon to be giving up car carriers, strollers, baby shades, baby hats, baby blankets, screaming toddlers. The woman in front of me at the library, the woman behind me at the Rite Aid, the woman next to me at the movies, the woman to my left as I wash my hands in the second-floor bathroom at Nordstrom's. Models popping babies, actresses popping babies, the teenager next door popping a baby, the middle-aged cashier at the Jiffy Mart popping a baby. Every woman in the universe spreading her legs wide and popping out a squinty-eyed, wrinkled-up, crusty-headed infant, no problem, no big deal, nothing no one's already done a million billion times before. Every woman everywhere, lifting her shirt to reveal huge, overloaded, milk-laden breasts, with huge brown elongated nipples. Milk spilling on shirts, on nighties, on little baby buntings. China, New Zealand, Ecuador, Sierra Leone. Every goddamn way you turn.

I tell my therapist all of this and he doesn't even shrug at the obviousness of it all. Or maybe he just doesn't know what to do with me anymore. Rather than pay him for nothing, I may as well spend an hour burning a hundred twenty-five dollar bills, one by one. Might be fun, actually. Might give me something to do.

What was all of it for, anyway? I ask him. Because if there was a reason for all of this, I'm not seeing it.

At this he shrugs. He hands me a tissue. Finally he speaks.

Julia, he says. It's a terrible thing that's happened to you. That's all.

17

The school year dwindles down. The last week is a joke. Between award assemblies and Field Day and end-of-the-year parties and the all-school lunchtime barbecue, there's not a mention of academics. I skip most of the festivities to pack up the resource room. It's occurred to me that I won't be coming back next year. Not that I have any great plans for the rest of my life. I don't even have any plans for the coming weekend. All I know is what I won't be doing. Won't be raising a baby. Won't be ignoring kids in the resource room. Won't be waiting for Ray to call. It's a start, anyway.

It seems as though all the people I know have made

one big circle and ended up exactly where they started. Bill moved back in with Gwen—she's making him sleep downstairs for now, on the fold-out couch. Elsa's shaved her pubic hair again. And I'm not planning any more un-planned pregnancies.

I suppose this is all progress of some sort.

Tina takes me to the seamstress to get my dress fitted for the wedding. We're all wearing black, except for Tina, who has chosen a lovely ivory dress covered with tiny beads. My dress is sleeveless, cut low in the front and tight at the waist, with a sweeping bottom that ends in a frantic ruffle around the ankles. It comes with pink gloves. I feel pretty stupid in the whole getup, but Tina insists it looks great. She's so high now with wedding plans that she can't see straight.

She wants to take me to lunch after the fitting, and I say all right, even though eating lunch is beyond my capa-bilities. But Tina looks so tiny and young, and she's so ex-cited about her life's trajectory—who am I to throw a wrench in her plans?

I order a chocolate milk shake, a Diet Coke, a cup of coffee, and a water. I do this only because it strikes me as hilarious in that moment, and it's been a while since some-thing has struck me as hilarious. Tina orders a salad.

My drinks arrive and I line them up in front of me, good little soldiers in the war against my unhappiness. How desperate to please they look! And then I glance up at Tina and see that she is desperate to please, too. This is what I have done to people. My existence makes them anxious.

I'm all right, I say. It's a time thing, you know?

And although I hate to admit it, even to myself, I know the truth of that simple statement. Fucking time, it never quits.

Relationship Test #5:

Your fifteenth wedding anniversary arrives. You call your husband at work. You say, Happy anniversary. He says, Happy anniversary, right back to you. You say, I just want to say thank you for ten really good years.

Your husband:

A. Laughs.

B. Laughs and says, That sounds about right.

C. Laughs and says, Amazing, isn't it?

My mother calls. She is a wreck. She doesn't know what to wear to Tina's wedding. What to do with her hair. How fancy the whole thing will be. Can she lose ten pounds in a month? What should she buy them for a present? What am I going to buy them? The world can fall to pieces, but some things never change. There's a bit of comfort in that, I suppose.

Then Jim's mom calls. She sounds quite chipper across the phone line. It's a courtesy call, a check-in. She never used to check in with me, but since the dead-baby thing, she's called a handful of times, never with anything to say. It's excruciating, but I know she needs the phone call, so I fill the space with dumb sentences. This time Alice wants to know how the fitting went. Did I like the dress? Was the length all right? Did Tina talk to me about the shoes? We spend our time going over these kinds of wedding details, so the conversation flows more smoothly than usual. Finally, though, we have squeezed our agenda dry. There is a moment of silence, and then Alice asks, How are you, dear?

I'm all right, I say.

There is another silence, during which I realize that I'm waiting for her to impart some kind of wisdom. It seems that she is about to tell me something I can really use, some piece of advice, some words that will ring true in my ears.

Okay, dear, she says. We'll talk again soon.

* * *

Gwen sleeps with Bill again. She comes over on a Sunday morning to tell me about it, still dressed in her raggedy brown robe, her hair pulled back in a hasty ponytail, a cigarette on her lips.

Same as ever, she says. Can't decide if that's a good thing or not.

I sleep with Jim again. I don't tell Gwen this, but for me, something is entirely different. I don't know how to explain it, exactly. It's kind of like when you come home after a long time away. It's still your house, your bed. Those are still your towels in the bathroom. Your things in the drawers. But somehow, now, you're ridiculously grateful to see them. God knows why, but you're relieved to see it all again.

We take Chad downtown to buy a suit for the wedding. We end up in a men's clothing shop, dealing with a thirtyish salesman drenched in some kind of sickly, manly smell, his hair cropped short against his head, his neck thick. He rubs his hands together a lot, as though he's been warned to always keep them in view. Together, we stroll the aisles, looking for something appropriate. Chad shakes his head at most of what is shown him, until at last he agrees to try on a blue jacket and gray slacks. He won't go any further than that. The salesman grabs a few more items, and we all head to the dressing rooms at the back of the store.

Jim is poking through the ties with the salesman, so he misses the moment when the curtain to Chad's dressing room falls open, and I catch Chad, half dressed in skivvies and dark socks. I haven't seen him in his underwear in years. He looks so darling, so fresh and young. I want to go into the dressing room with him, help him dress, the way I used to do. I want to hug him close. I want him to hug me back. Just then, Chad looks up and horror crosses his face, as he sees me seeing him.

God, Mom, he says, pulling the curtain closed.

Jim shows me a couple of ties he's considering for himself, and I tell him the green one, because of his eyes.

Really? he says.

Get what you want, I say.

The green one, you think?

He pulls the green tie from the rack and inspects its pattern.

Well, this one's all right, too, I say, drawing out his other pick, a light-gray number with burgundy fish swimming in rows across it.

No, you were right the first time, Jim says. He tosses the green tie around my neck. Holding on to each end, he draws me in close.

Taking me prisoner, are you? I ask.

Yes, he says, and kisses me there in the back of the store, while the salesman pretends not to notice.

And then Ray does call. He wants to know how the pregnancy's going. Wants me to remind him of my due date.

August, I tell him.

That's right, he says.

Except that I lost the baby.

You what?

I lost the baby. I had a miscarriage.

What? When? My God, I'm so sorry.

It's all right. It's been a while now, anyway.

Julia. I'm really, really sorry.

Yeah.

So how's everything else? he asks.

There really isn't anything else.

I'll be up there in the fall, he says. Probably bad timing to say this, but Melissa and Greg are pregnant.

Great, I say. That's really great. Thanks for letting me know.

The wedding is strange at first, divided up as it is into mostly black people on the groom's side of the aisle and mostly white people on the bride's. Aside from the color thing, though, people look pretty much the same, depending on their decade. The older men are all wearing suits and ties, and the older women are all in nice, conservative outfits with nylons and sensible shoes. The younger women—Tina's friends—have taken the cleavage theme seriously. Breasts are everywhere, along with lots of legs and great haircuts. Their outfits I can't get a take on— somewhere there is a thread that ties them all together, but I am too old to find it. Maybe it's just youth, looking utterly fabulous on the young.

I walk down the aisle with Brian's older brother, Gary. He has Brian's tiny ears and perfect teeth, but he's almost a foot taller, which is a good thing since the shoes Tina picked for her bridesmaids have thin, high spikes, which make me feel as though I were reeling off into space. As we pass Chad and Jim, Chad gives me a big thumbs-up, which is soaked in sarcasm, but which he really means at the same time. Jim smiles, reaches out to brush my arm with his fingertips, and misses. I get his point anyway.

Tina has never looked so beautiful. She stands next to Brian, holding his hands while they take their vows. The room is silent but for their quiet voices, promising a future together. I hold my breath and listen.

Huge thanks to Janet Dorfman and Robin Simons; to my fabulous agent, Sarah Burnes; and to my sharp and patient editor, Aimee Taub. Many thanks also to Anna Jardine, Jessica Craig, Arlo Crawford, Kitty Goldston, Marilynn Gottlieb, Sarah Crichton, Nancy Blakey, Ellen Wright Berdinner, Eric Hoffman, Frank Walker, John Marshall, and the staff at the Bainbridge Island Public Library, where much of this book was written.

Big kisses and deep gratitude to Hannah and Gillon Crichton.

Finally, endless thanks to the most generous man on the planet, my husband, Rob Crichton.

Readers Guide to

We are all fine here

Discussion Questions

1. Missed opportunity is a major theme in Julia's life. In one scene, she reprimands a dead fly on her windowsill for not flying when it had the chance. Although missed opportunity does not literally represent deathly consequences for Julia, what psychological consequences does she deal with?

2. What factors contribute to Julia's obsession with Ray? Do you have to love someone to be obsessed with them?

3. At one point, Julia suggests that every young wife fantasizes about her husband getting killed so she can be "young and beautiful, and, even more than that, tragic." On the surface, this is Julia's humor at its darkest—but how would you further interpret this bold statement in terms of basic human dilemmas?

4. About halfway through the novel, Julia attempts—and fails—to describe her "perfect Saturday" because she realizes that she doesn't know what she wants. Do you feel that you have a better sense of what Julia wants than she seems to? What advice would you give if you were one of Julia's close friends?

5. Sprinkled through the narrative are five "relationship tests." What purpose do they serve in the story? Did you find yourself answering for Julia? For yourself? For both?

6. Ray and Chad are male figures who are very important to Julia despite the fact that Ray rarely calls and Chad evolves from being an affectionate boy to a remote teenager. Julia is able to tolerate the distance between herself and Chad much better than she handles the distance between herself and Ray. Other than her motherly bond, what makes her level of tolerance for Chad's absence possible?

7. Julia finds a sense of solace and companionship in her friends Elsa and Gwen, at times divulging big secrets to them that she is reluctant to share with Jim. What are the main obstacles between Julia and Jim?

8. Julia seems to be trying to push Ray away when she tells him he isn't the baby's father. Were you surprised when

Julia subsequently chooses to call Ray when she has her scare? Why or why not?

9. When Julia becomes pregnant, things start to change— not only for her, but for Jim as well. It's been said that individuals rise to the occasion when faced with a challenge or crisis. To what degree is this true of Julia and Jim?

10. The phrase "we are all fine here" comes from Julia's mother, who tends to gloss over the rough spots in life. Compare Julia's attitude with her mother's.

11. Tom, Julia's coworker, briefly gets back together with his ex-girlfriend. Chad and Tricia break up, then get back together. Gwen and her husband separate, then get back together. Tina, Jim's sister, stops fooling around and gets engaged. Patricia, Jim's coworker, leaves her husband and then has an office affair. Elsa leaves her husband, and then goes back to him. Given the crazy-quilt of relationship patterns that make up *We Are All Fine Here*, what conclusions can be drawn about life and love?

12. Look into Julia's future. Are she and Jim still together?